"From The Minute I Showed Up Here I've Rubbed You The Wrong Way."

Harper stared at him in helpless fascination. This was the Ashton Croft she'd been dying to get to know. The dashing adventurer who'd gamely hiked into dangerous surroundings to share a meal with locals and educate his viewers about what was unique to the area. It was always fascinating and often stuck with her long after the credits rolled.

"If you knew that, why didn't you try rubbing me the right way?" Harper regretted the words the instant they left her lips. They sounded like flirtatious banter. "What I meant was..."

Ashton shook his head, stopping her flow of words. A low chuckle vibrated in his chest. "Please don't try to explain it," he said. "I think it's the first honest thing you've ever said to me."

* * *

A Taste of Temptation is part of the Las Vegas Nights trilogy: Where love is the biggest gamble of all!

* * *

If you're on Twitter,
tell us what you think of Harlequin Desire!
#harlequindesire

Dear Reader,

Being a huge fan of cooking shows, it was only a matter of time before I had a chef as a hero. A man who knows his way around a kitchen is oh-so-sexy. And when he's also an adventure-loving world traveler, I'm hooked.

Researching new places to visit is a favorite pastime of mine. I'd never considered South Africa a must-see destination until I started researching the perfect safari camp for Harper and Ashton to fall in love. As I wrote, I listened to sounds of the bush, and by the time I finished the story I felt as if I'd actually traveled there. The area's culture and history intrigue me, and I've added South Africa to my growing list of places I'd like to experience.

I hope you enjoy this third installment of my Las Vegas Nights series featuring the Fontaine sisters. I certainly had a blast writing their stories. I always enjoy hearing from my readers. You can contact me at cat.schield@yahoo.com.

All the best,

Cat Schield

A TASTE OF
TEMPTATION

—

CAT SCHIELD

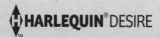

Recycling programs
for this product may
not exist in your area.

ISBN-13: 978-0-373-73327-9

A TASTE OF TEMPTATION

Printed in U.S.A.

CAT SCHIELD

has been reading and writing romance since high school. Although she graduated from college with a B.A. in business, her idea of a perfect career was writing books for Harlequin. And now, after winning the Romance Writers of America 2010 Golden Heart Award for series contemporary romance, that dream has come true. Cat lives in Minnesota with her daughter, Emily, and their Burmese cat. When she's not writing sexy, romantic stories for Harlequin Desire, she can be found sailing with friends on the St. Croix River, or in more exotic locales, like the Caribbean and Europe. She loves to hear from readers. Find her at www.catschield.com. Follow her on Twitter, @catschield.

To my MFW-BIAW Golden Girls: Nan Dixon,
Lizbeth Selvig and Nancy Holland.
Thanks for keeping me motivated and inspired.
You ladies rock.

One

As soon as Harper Fontaine stepped from her lively casino into her stylish new restaurant, she checked near the door for a rolling black leather duffel. Ashton Croft's *go* bag. She loathed the thing. It represented everything that drove her crazy about the celebrity chef. His tendency to show up without warning. The way he thrived on excitement, and when none could be found, his knack for either stirring it up or heading out of town on some adventure or another.

But she needed the bag to be there because it would mean that Ashton had shown up for today's head chef interview. Batouri's grand opening was two weeks away. When the original deadline for the opening of the restaurant had come and gone without it being ready, Harper had questioned the wisdom of asking an unreliable television personality to start a restaurant in her hotel.

True, the buzz about the grand opening had drawn all eyes and scads of publicity to her hotel, Fontaine Ciel, but was the attention worth the stress Ashton had heaped on those in charge of making the restaurant a success? Carlo Perrault, the restaurant's manager, wasn't sleeping and had grown irritable these past two months. Harper was grinding her teeth at night. The headaches induced by this behavior had forced to her seek medical help. She now wore a mouth guard when she went to bed. Slipping the awkward plastic device into her mouth, she would lie on the mattress and wish she had some idea what happened to Ashton's initial enthusiasm about the restaurant.

The longer the filming of *The Culinary Wanderer* had gone in Indonesia, the more difficult she'd found working with him to be. They'd had to postpone Batouri's launch date twice because of scheduling conflicts with his travels for his wildly popular television series.

Which was why Harper refused to delay again. The restaurant's black floors were polished. The chandeliers had been hung from the high cove ceiling. Their light illuminated the white napkins and crystal wine goblets on the black tables. Ten days earlier the painters had completed the metallic gold treatment on the three wide pillars down the center of the room. Near the fully stocked bar, the assistant manager was putting the waitstaff through their paces.

But for two things, Batouri was ready to open. Two key things. It lacked a head chef and a menu.

And seeing that Ashton's *go* bag wasn't in its usual place, it looked as if that menu was going to have to wait. Harper glanced at her watch. It was exactly four in the afternoon. She'd told Ashton the interview would happen at three to make certain he arrived on time. Playing these sorts of games wasn't in her nature, but she was at her wits' end in dealing with the celebrity chef.

She dialed her assistant. Mary picked up on the second ring.

Harper got straight to business. "Did Ashton Croft call to say he'd be delayed?"

"No."

"And his plane was supposed to land in Las Vegas at one?"

"Yes, I confirmed his itinerary this morning."

Damn the man. Two weeks ago Ashton had promised Harper his full attention starting today. She should have known better. "Thank you, Mary. Let me know if you hear from him."

"Sure thing." Harper was on the verge of disconnecting the call when something Mary said caught her attention. "…in your office."

Carlo Perrault emerged from the kitchen, a scowl on his handsome face. The forty-six-year-old restaurant manager was known for his composure, but even he was showing signs of stress at all the things that still needed to be done. "We have a problem."

"I'm sorry, Mary. Who did you say was in my office?"

"Your mother."

"My mother?" Surprise kept her from guarding her tone. Aware of Carlo's scrutiny, Harper turned her back on him and stepped away to give herself some semblance of privacy. "Did she say what she was doing in Vegas?"

"No, but she seems upset."

"Just upset?" Harper mused.

Penelope Fontaine wouldn't have left her elegant condo in Boca Raton to fly two thousand miles to visit Harper unless something was seriously wrong. And if it was, why had Penelope come to Harper? Usually Penelope took her problems to her father-in-law, Henry Fontaine.

"You once mentioned she smokes when she's agitated," Mary said. "She's starting her second cigarette."

"She's smoking in my office?" Harper pinched the bridge of her nose. She wanted to insist Mary tell her mother to put out the cigarette, but knew that would be asking too much of her assistant. "I'll be there in five minutes."

"You can't leave," Carlo protested. "Croft has started the interview without you."

"Great," she muttered. "How long has he been here?"

"Long enough to taste everything Chef Cole has prepared." Carlo's dour expression was enough to tell Harper that this interview was going the way the other seven had.

"Mary, looks like I am going to be a while. Get my mother settled in a suite and I'll visit her as soon as I'm done here." Harper hung up and turned to Carlo. "If he messes this interview up, I'm going to kill him."

Carlo offered her a tight nod of understanding.

The hostility in the two male voices hit her before she'd reached the food pass area.

"There's nothing wrong with the sear on these scallops," one of the men protested, his tone both arrogant and simmering with hostility. "And the sauce is not under seasoned."

"It's obvious the only thing worse than your culinary skills is your wretched palate."

Pain stabbed Harper's temple as she recognized the voice of the second speaker. Ashton Croft had been interviewing head chefs for two months, rejecting one after another for failing to live up to his exacting standards.

Harper snapped her vertebrae into a stiff line and stepped into the meticulously organized, stainless-steel kitchen. As was her habit, her gaze swung immediately to Ashton. He dominated the room with his presence. Tall and imposing in his chef whites, he stood glaring at Chef Cole, muscular arms crossed over his broad chest.

He hadn't yet noticed her, hadn't turned his Persian-blue eyes her way, hadn't noted her slight breathlessness. His passion for food sent his innate charisma soaring. She cursed the hero worship that she couldn't completely squash despite her professionalism. She was unequal parts frustrated with the restaurateur and enamored of the dashing adventurer.

His travels fascinated her. Some of the things Ashton had eaten made Harper shudder, but he boldly consumed whatever he was offered. She'd spend her entire life knowing exactly where she was going, and the way he allowed random opportunities to push him into unexpected and sometimes startling discoveries both unnerved and captivated her. Watching his television shows had made her realize just how safe her world was. And a seed of restlessness had sprouted inside her.

With effort Harper ripped her gaze from Ashton and turned her attention to the other chef. Taking in the interviewee's blazing eyes and clenched fists, she donned her most diplomatic expression and entered the war zone.

"Good afternoon, gentlemen." She stepped into the middle of the clash with calm authority. She wanted Chef Dillon Cole to run Batouri's kitchen. He was an excellent chef as well as a strong, organized leader. Harper restrained a weary sigh. Of all the candidates, he'd been Harper's first choice for head chef. It was why she'd saved his interview until the last. This close to the restaurant's already delayed grand opening, she had the leverage she needed to force Ashton's hand. "I stopped by to see how things are going."

"Taste this," Ashton commanded, pushing the plate in her direction without ever taking his eyes off Cole. "Tell me if you think it's up to Batouri standards."

The first time he'd done this she'd been flattered that he wanted her opinion. After the third candidate had been rejected, she'd realized he was merely using her to drive home a point. If someone with no culinary experience could taste the inferior quality of the entrées, the chef who'd prepared the dish had failed.

Harper made no move to do as he'd asked. "May I speak to you privately for a moment?"

"Can it wait?" Ashton never took his eyes off Chef Cole.

She fought to keep her frustration on a tight leash. How would it play out on social media if the general manager of Fontaine Ciel was recorded shrieking empty threats at the famous Chef Croft?

"No."

Her conviction came through loud and clear, snagging Ashton's complete attention. His laser-sharp blue eyes scanned her expression. Sexual interest flared low in her belly. It traveled upward, leaving every nerve it touched sizzling with anticipation. She cursed silently. Her body's tendency to overreact to the man's rakish good looks and raw masculinity had distracted her all too often. She was not her professional best around him.

Once again Harper reminded herself that the flesh and blood man standing before her was unreliable and unconcerned with how his priorities impacted those around him. The dashing adventurer he portrayed on television was entertaining to watch as he charmed locals by listening attentively to their stories and sampling the regional specialties. But when it came to the routine matters necessary to start a restaurant, he easily became distracted.

Lips tightening, Ashton nodded. "Excuse us," he said to Chef Cole, and gestured for Harper to return to the dining room. "What's so important?" he demanded as soon as they'd exited the kitchen.

"The restaurant opens in two weeks."

"I'm aware of that."

"The press releases have gone out. There will be no further postponement."

"Understood."

She tamped down her irritation. "We need a head chef."

"I will take charge of the kitchen."

If only that were true. "I need someone I can rely on to be here every day."

His nod indicated he saw where she was going. "You want me to hire Cole."

"The last time I was in Chicago I ate at his restaurant. It was excellent. I was looking forward to tasting what he'd created today."

"You didn't miss much."

Harper spent a minute studying Ashton. There was something different about him today. Usually he breezed in, found something wrong with the construction or the fixtures and then stirred up everyone associated with the project before coming up with a fix for whatever he perceived wrong. Working with him had been stressful and invigorating, but in the end the restaurant was far better for his interference.

Today he seemed to be creating trouble for the sake of drama rather than because he had real issues with Chef Cole.

"Is there something going on with you?"

Her abrupt change in topic startled him into a moment of uncertainty. "Not a thing. Why?"

"Because you were on time for a change."

"I believe I was an hour early."

She gestured toward the door, making no effort to correct him. "And there's no *go* bag."

"*Go* bag?" he echoed.

"The black leather bag that you bring with you everywhere."

"You mean my rolling duffel?" He pointed toward a far corner of the restaurant where the bag sat beside a semicircular corner booth. "Why do you call it a *go* bag?"

"Because it's your crutch."

Amusement narrowed his eyes. "My crutch."

"When things get too tedious you make some excuse, grab the bag and head off in search of greater excitement."

"Leaving you behind to clean up after me?"

She let a brief silence answer his question. "You've interviewed and rejected seven head chef candidates."

He cocked an eyebrow. "What's your point?"

"I need you to hire someone. Chef Cole is that person."

"You didn't taste his entrées." When it came to food, Ashton was a creative genius. She wasn't surprised he couldn't find someone who was capable of living up to his demanding criteria. "I found them lacking."

"He has the experience and the organization to run this kitchen the way I expect it to be run—"

Ashton interrupted. "When you came to me about opening a restaurant in your hotel, I thought you understood that I had the last and final word on all creative."

"Creative, yes, but this is about the management of the kitchen." Which was why she was determined to get her way. She'd been able to control costs and manage the construction schedule, working hard to manifest Ashton's vision for the restaurant without exceeding budget.

In that respect their working relationship meshed.

"But the kitchen is where the magic happens."

"Except there's no magic happening because we don't have a menu or a head chef to work with the kitchen staff." Pain shot through her head. She winced.

"We will be ready for the opening." His absolute confidence should have shut down all her worries.

"But—"

"Trust me." His deep voice broke into her protest, his soothing cadence catching her off guard.

"I do." That's not what she'd meant to say.

But she knew it was true. They might have had completely different philosophies on how to accomplish something, but he had proven time and again he was as capable of getting things done as she. Deep down she knew he'd plan a fantastic menu and win the love of customers and critics alike.

That it would happen in the frantic last hours before the door opened was what made her crazy.

Famous dimples flashing, he countered, "No, you don't. From the minute I showed up here I've rubbed you the wrong way."

Harper stared at him in helpless fascination. This was the Ashton Croft she'd been dying to get to know. The man who charmed smiles from people who'd seen nothing but hardship and violence. The dashing adventurer who'd on occasion gamely hiked into dangerous surroundings to share a meal with locals and educate his viewers about what was unique to the area. It was always intriguing and often stuck with her long after the credits rolled.

"If you knew that, why didn't you try rubbing me the right way?" Harper regretted the words the instant they left her lips. They sounded like flirtatious banter. "What I meant was…"

Ashton shook his head, stopping her flow of words.

Not once since they'd first met nine months ago had she given him any hint that her interest in him went beyond his skills in the kitchen. Plagued by unruly flashes of lust for the überprofessional businesswoman and not wanting anything to interfere with the negotiations for the Las Vegas restaurant, he'd ignored his disobedient hormones and kept things strictly business.

But as they neared the date for the restaurant opening, he found it harder and harder to stop seeing her as an attractive—if too serious—woman.

It made him crazy that he couldn't accept that she wasn't interested and move on. This was Vegas. There were thousands of women arriving every day looking to have a good time. Perfect for a frequent flier like him. He rarely stayed in the same location for more than a few days. The time he'd spent in Vegas these past few months was the most settled he'd been since leaving New York City ten years earlier.

A low chuckle vibrated his chest. "Please don't try to explain it," he said. "I think it's the first honest thing you've ever said to me."

"That's not true." But she went no further.

"I think it is."

Ashton had watched her walking the line between frustration and diplomacy with finesse and grace these many months. He wasn't completely oblivious to how hard he'd made her life.

At the beginning of the project he'd been excited to put his creative stamp on Las Vegas. He hadn't understood until it was too late how difficult his ideas would be to communicate. He'd demanded changes that irritated the designers and caused forward progress to halt. Forced by his filming timeline to oversee the restaurant from thousands of miles away, he'd found few things that met with his approval. The layout of the kitchen wasn't to his satisfaction. Numerous shipments of lighting and furniture samples didn't meet his expectations.

Then there were the filming delays caused by the Indonesian weather. Days of rain threw off their schedule. The crew joked that their ratings would skyrocket if they captured him soaked through, his clothes plastered to his body, but no one wanted to venture out into the mud and damp.

"Why don't I tell Cole he blew the interview and then fix something delicious. You can tell me what's bothering you while we eat."

"The lack of a head chef is what's bothering me."

"There has to be something else. You're not usually so testy."

"I'm not testy. I simply don't have time to eat with you."

"Five minutes ago you were ready to sit down and taste everything Cole had prepared." He crossed his arms and regarded her solemnly. "So I have to ask, what is it about my food you don't like?"

"It's not your food. I ate at Turinos while you were executive chef and the food was brilliant. You don't seriously think I'd invite you to open a restaurant here if I didn't love your cooking."

"Then is it me you don't like?" He held up his hand to forestall her denial. "I've been told I can be difficult to work with."

She took a deep breath and let it out, releasing some of the tension. "You've been murder to work with, but I think the restaurant's going to be worth every name I've called you."

Her bluntness made the corners of his mouth twitch. "You've called me names?"

"Never where anyone could hear me."

"Of course."

"Meaning?"

"Just that you're too much of a lady to ever let loose."

"And there's something wrong with being a lady?"

In the back of his mind a rational voice warned that he was baiting her. At the beginning of their association he'd often lobbed provocative statements her way. But she'd been far too professional to react and eventually he'd stopped aggravating her. This conversation felt different. As if she'd let the mask slide and was giving him a taste of her true self.

"Only that you never seem to have any fun."

She wasn't the only one who'd done her homework. He knew about the contest she was waging against her half sisters to one day take over as CEO of the family business. She'd had a phenomenal amount of success in her career, but Harper wasn't one to rest on her past achievements. In that way, they were alike. No one could put as much pressure on Harper as she put on herself.

"I have a great deal riding on the success of my hotel." She wouldn't stop until she had everything exactly the way she wanted it. "And you aren't one to talk. You barely take any time off between filming *The Culinary Wanderer,* promoting the series and managing your other restaurants."

"I won't deny that I'm busy, but I also take time to enjoy what I'm doing." He cocked his head. "Do you?"

"I enjoy my work. I wouldn't be doing it if I didn't." But beneath her vehemence was a grain of doubt.

She'd tried to hide her weariness with a careful application of concealer and blush, but he'd watched her long hours bite deeper into her energy each time he came to check on the restaurant's progress.

"But there must be something for you besides work," he said. "What's something you've always wanted to do but haven't gotten around to yet?"

"You make it sound like I'm sacrificing everything for my career."

In fact, he hadn't been saying that at all, but that she chose to interpret his question this way told him more than she'd intended.

"Everyone has dreams of something carefree and fun they'd like to do someday."

"I agree."

"Tell me one of yours."

"I don't get the point."

Was she stalling? Trying to come up with something safe? "Humor me. What's the first thing that pops into your mind?"

With her brows drawn together in exasperation, she blurted out, "I'd like to ride a camel across the desert and sleep in a tent."

Ashton wasn't sure which of them was more surprised by her outburst. "Seriously?" He laughed. "That's not at all what I expected you to say. I thought you'd tell me you wanted to…" He trailed off. They'd worked together for nine months and he knew so little about her.

"Wanted to what?" she prompted, wary curiosity in her warm brown eyes.

"I'm not sure. You aren't the sort of woman I imagine wanting to run off to Paris on a shopping spree or lounge on a yacht." She was too driven by timetables to enjoy such frivolous pursuits. "Maybe something more serious-minded. A visit to a museum, perhaps?"

His suggestion didn't meet with her approval. "You

know, I'm a little tired of everyone criticizing me for being too serious."

Whoa, he'd definitely touched a nerve there. "Who is everyone?"

"My family. My classmates when I was in school. Friends. Life isn't all about play, you know." She glanced down at her smartphone and frowned.

"It's also not all about work."

Sharp irritation sliced through her voice. "Says the man who rarely does any."

"Well, well, well." He flashed her a big grin. "That's some hellcat you keep bottled up."

She stared at him in consternation before sputtering, "That's ridiculous. There's no hellcat here."

"You didn't see the bloodlust in your eyes just now."

Her jaw worked as if she was grinding something particularly nasty between her teeth. "I'll admit to being a little on edge. You are not the easiest man to work with."

"Maybe not work with," he agreed. "But when you're ready to have some fun, give me a call."

In the quiet of the restaurant, Harper stared at Ashton with raised brows and lips softly parted. His offer wasn't sexual in nature, but when he spied the hope that flickered in her melted-chocolate eyes, his perception of her shifted dramatically.

"I don't have time—"

"For fun." He scrutinized her expression. "Yes, so you've said."

As a teenager, he'd fallen in with some dangerous criminals. Learning to read micro expressions had helped him survive. That he'd not picked up on the passionate woman concealed beneath Harper's professional exterior pointed out just how complacent he'd become.

Time to wake up and start paying attention.

She cleared her throat. "Getting back to Chef Cole…"

"I'll hire him if you spend an evening with me." This time he was deliberately hitting on her.

She set her hands on her hips and scowled at him. "Five minutes ago you were ready to pass on him."

"Five minutes ago I didn't realize just how starved for adventure you were."

"I'm very happy right where I am."

"When the first thing on your bucket list is riding a camel in the desert and sleeping in a tent, forgive me if I don't believe your life is as satisfying as you'd have people believe."

"I don't have a bucket list," she retorted. "And if I did, that wouldn't be the first thing on it. It was just something that popped into my head. I remember you doing that in an episode of *The Culinary Wanderer*."

"You're a fan?"

"Before I get into business with someone I do my research."

Sensible. But he hoped that hadn't been her only motivation. Swept by the urge to see her let her hair down, literally and figuratively, he decided to ignore her verbal cues and concentrate on what she was saying with her body.

"And your research involved watching my shows? I would have thought you'd be more interested in hard facts such as the financials of my four other restaurants and the uptick in advertising revenue my show brings to the network."

"All those things paint a very positive picture of you. I also spoke with a number of your employees and several of the crew who worked with you on your shows. As I said, I do my research."

Obviously she knew much more about him than he knew about her. The imbalance bothered him. "Then you know the sort of businessman I am, and when I say I'm willing to hire a chef you favor, it's not done lightly."

With her gaze firmly attached to his left shoulder, she murmured, "In exchange for a night with me."

"I proposed an evening." He couldn't help but laugh at the conclusion she'd jumped to. "You have a naughty mind if you think I'd barter hiring Cole for sex."

Hot color flared in her cheeks. "That's not what I was thinking."

"Oh, I think it was. I told you that hellcat was going to get you into trouble."

"I misspoke."

"I don't think so." Now that she was off balance, he decided to keep her that way. "I think it was a Freudian slip. You want me. You just can't admit it."

"What I want is for you to hire a chef and get him trained to your exacting standards so I don't have to worry about what happens after you leave."

She'd taken refuge in exasperation, but it wasn't fooling him.

"My offer still stands. Give me one evening and I'll hire Cole."

"Why would you want to spend an evening with me?" She looked as frazzled as he'd ever seen her.

"I thought you'd be interested in tasting the dishes I'm considering for the restaurant."

Her eyes narrowed. "And that's all there is to it?"

"Of course."

She regarded him in silence for several heartbeats before replying. "Hire Cole. You need someone accomplished to run your kitchen while you're off playing celebrity." With that, she pivoted on her conservative black pumps and strode across to his bag. Snagging the handle, she pulled it after her. "I'm taking this as collateral," she called over her shoulder.

It was a silly gesture—taking his clothes hostage wouldn't prevent him from getting on a plane—and so unlike Harper, the consummate professional. Ashton's gaze followed her, appreciating the pronounced sway of her hips. Thinking she'd put one over on him had injected a trace of strut into her stride.

"I will hire him," Ashton promised her. "And you will spend the evening with me."

"Sampling your menu." Her words floated back to him.

He'd been right about the hellcat lurking beneath her skin. It had been asleep far too long and he was the perfect guy to rouse it.

His final shot chased her out of the restaurant. "I'm going to make it a night you'll never forget."

Two

Smugness from her encounter with Ashton lasted about a second as she strode out of the restaurant and headed toward her office. What had she been thinking to walk off with his luggage? He must think she'd gone mad.

Well, hadn't she?

She'd agreed to an evening with him. Harper had no doubt she'd signed on for more than a private tasting of his menu. Which meant she was in big trouble. Already her mouth watered at the prospect of being the beneficiary of his culinary prowess. As long as that was the only prowess he plied her with, she might survive the evening without making a fool of herself. If he decided to test her level of resistance to his manly charms she wasn't going to maintain her professionalism very long.

Her skin burned as she thought of how he'd called her on her assumption that he wanted sex in exchange for hiring the chef she preferred. Not once had she suspected Ashton was the sort of man to make such a sordid offer. So why had she jumped to that conclusion? Even worse, why had she lobbed the accusation at him? Naturally, he'd presumed her misunderstanding represented her deepest desires.

And he was probably right. For the past nine months she'd been complaining that the real Ashton Croft wasn't as wonderful as the one on television. But that wasn't exactly true. His persona on TV was charismatic and amusing. He was the cool guy everyone wanted to hang out with. The flesh and blood Ashton Croft was no less appealing. It was just that the travel series didn't fully convey the masculine energy of the man. The rawness of his sex appeal.

Most of the time she focused on how frustrating he was. She was terrified of being bamboozled by his dimples and rakish grin. If he had any idea how easily he could knock her socks off, he'd probably go after a few other items of clothing, as well.

Harper shook her head at the thought. She was not going to sleep with Ashton Croft. It would be different if they'd met in some exotic locale; she could see herself being one of his random hook ups. The next morning, she would chalk up the evening as an adventure worth having. Hadn't she spent tedious hours on the treadmill imagining all sorts of spicy scenarios where she bumped into Ashton at a vineyard in Tuscany or on a walk around Dubrovnik's ancient city walls? There they would share a sunset and he'd persuade her to join him for dinner. On a private terrace overlooking the Adriatic Sea and surrounded by candles, he'd take her into his arms and…

The faint smell of cigarette smoke ripped Harper from her daydream.

Parking Ashton's *go* bag just inside the door of her office, Harper surveyed her formerly pristine sanctuary. Her mother's ostrich leather Burberry holdall sat on the sky-blue sofa, half the contents scattered around it. An empty pack of cigarettes lay crushed on the coffee table beside a crystal tumbler with a pale pink lipstick stain. The elegant lines of a cream trench coat were draped over Harper's executive chair. Her mother had definitely moved in.

Penelope Fontaine stood by the window overlooking the Las Vegas strip, her right hand resting at her throat, as if protecting the string of large black pearls she wore. A thin tendril of smoke rose from the cigarette pinched between the fingers of her other hand. In a black-and-white Chanel dress, with her long blond hair pulled away from her face in a classic chignon, she looked elegant and untouchable.

The sight stirred up memories of the day her parents had sat her down and explained that they were splitting up. Her mother needed to move to Florida for her health. Harper would remain in New York City with her father. Which basically meant she'd be alone with the staff because Ross Fontaine had spent most of his time avoiding the company's New York headquarters and his father's expectations. With Fontaine Hotels and Resorts' extensive holdings in the U.S. and abroad, Harper's father could be as irresponsible as he wanted without Henry Fontaine being the wiser.

"Mother, I would appreciate it if you didn't smoke in my office." Harper advanced toward Penelope, ready to pluck the cigarette from her mother if she didn't comply.

"I'm sorry, Harper." Crossing to the coffee table, she dropped the cigarette into the empty glass. "You know how I revert when I'm upset."

The lingering smell of smoke made Harper's nose tingle unpleasantly. "What's bothering you?" She fetched a can of air freshener from one of the cabinets that lined the east wall and sprayed the room with ocean breezes.

"I need your help." Penelope's voice warbled as she spoke the last word.

Unsure whether her mother was being theatrical or if she was truly in trouble, Harper took a quick inventory. Penelope's eyes looked like a forest after a downpour, the green enhanced by the redness that rimmed them.

"You've been crying." This was no bid for her daughter's attention. "What's wrong?"

"Something terrible has happened." Harper heard the weight of the world in Penelope's voice. "Why else do you think I came to this godforsaken city? It's not as if you'd come visit me in Florida."

"The hotel is taking all my energy right now." Harper knew better than to book passage on her mother's guilt trip, but her encounter with Ashton had stirred up her emotions. "Why didn't you go to Grandfather?"

Penelope fiddled with the ten-carat diamond she wore on her left hand despite her husband's death five years earlier. Why would she take if off now when she'd worn the ring through eighteen years of being separated from Ross Fontaine?

"Henry can't help me with this."

"But I can?" Harper struggled to get her head around this shift in her world's axis.

Never once had her mother reached out like this. Penelope was of the mindset that only men could solve the world's problems. Women were supposed to adorn their husbands' arms, looking beautiful and displaying graceful manners. They weren't supposed to run billion-dollar corporations at the expense of attracting lovers, much less suitable husbands.

"You're the only one who can."

All her life Harper had been waiting for her mother to acknowledge her as powerful and capable. That Penelope had turned to her daughter for help was as thrilling a victory as Harper had ever known. "What do you need?"

"Money."

Her mother received a sizeable allowance each month from the Fontaine family trust. What could she possibly need to buy that she couldn't turn to Harper's grandfather? "Why?"

"I'm being blackmailed."

Blackmailed? This was the last thing Harper expected to hear.

"Have you spoken to the police?" To Harper's mind, paying a blackmailer was never a good idea.

Penelope stared at Harper as if she'd suggested her mother get a job. "This is private business."

"Blackmail is illegal."

"I will not have my personal affairs become public knowledge."

Until her mother had retreated to Florida, Harper had been conditioned daily to believe that image was everything. And even though she'd subsequently found her true strength lay in being resourceful and focused, that earlier rhetoric wasn't easily ignored.

"I understand your reputation means everything to you, but what's to say the blackmailer won't leak the information even though you pay him?"

"He's promised not to." Penelope said this as if stunned that her daughter could be that stupid. "I came here thinking you'd help me."

Harper chewed on a sigh before saying, "How much do you need?"

"Three hundred and fifty thousand dollars."

The sum rendered Harper speechless for a long moment. "What did you do?"

Treating her mother with such bluntness wasn't going to win Harper any points, but the amount had caught her off guard.

Penelope gathered outrage around her like a shawl. "That's none of your concern."

"Excuse me for interrupting." Ashton strode into the room, looking far from remorseful that he'd barged in.

Too stunned by the bomb her mother had dropped to react to his intrusion, Harper sat motionless and watched him approach. His gaze shifted from her to Penelope, and Harper wondered if he was comparing mother and daughter.

Was he making the assumption that Harper and her mother were the same? Wealthy women, confident in their identity, knowing exactly how their lives were going to play out and content with the direction. Most days that's how Harper felt. Not today.

"Harper?" her mother's low warning tone prodded Harper to her feet.

"Mother, this is Chef Ashton Croft. He is the creative genius behind Batouri. Ashton, this is my mother, Penelope Fontaine."

She ignored the flash of humor in Ashton's eyes as she introduced him as a creative genius. It was true. No matter how big a pain in the ass he'd been, there was no denying the man was brilliant in the kitchen.

"Delighted to meet you," Penelope murmured, extending her hand like a queen to her subject.

Harper mentally rolled her eyes as Ashton clasped her mother's hand and flashed his charismatic celebrity grin.

"I've enjoyed working with your daughter."

Liar.

He'd tolerated her at best.

Seeing the effect his dazzling persona was having on her mother, Harper momentarily surrendered to amusement. Not normally one to be charmed by a handsome face or flirtation, Penelope appeared as if she'd forgotten all about the blackmail that had driven her more than two thousand miles to seek her daughter's help.

As much as she hated interrupting their mutual love fest, Harper wanted to return to her mother's blackmail problem and get the issue solved. "Is there something you needed from me?" she asked Ashton.

His attention swung to her. "Just my laptop. I have a video conference in ten minutes."

"It's over there." She gestured toward the black bag.

He bent to a side pocket in the duffel and took out a thin silver computer. Harper followed the smooth bunch and flex of his muscles, and her breath hissed out in appreciation. Strong and athletic in his cargo pants, denim shirt and hiking boots, sun-streaked shaggy hair falling into his bright blue eyes, he represented everything that Harper was not. Physical, unpredictable, exciting. The yang to her yin, she realized, and felt heat rise in her cheeks.

"Leave the bag," she commanded, her voice a husky blur. "I'm not done with you yet."

The corner of his mouth kicked up. "Of course."

She caught his smug gaze and stared him down in silence, refusing to backpedal or stumble through an explanation of what she'd actually meant. And maybe just a little afraid to ask herself about the subtext he'd picked up on.

"Check with Mary to see which conference room is available."

"I appreciate the accommodation."

"Come see me when you're done. I'm interested to hear how your conversation with Chef Cole went."

"I look forward to telling you. Will you be here?"

Harper glanced at her mother. "I'm not certain where I'll be. Ask Mary. She has a knack for finding me."

He nodded and exited her office. With his departure, the energy level in the room plummeted. Harper's heart pounded in her chest as if she'd done a two-minute sprint on her treadmill.

"You're letting that scruffy man open a restaurant in your hotel?"

Penelope's criticism would've stung if Harper hadn't witnessed her mother batting her eyelash extensions at *that scruffy man* only moments before. "He only recently returned from four months in Indonesia."

"I thought you said he was a chef. What was he doing there?"

"Filming his television series, *The Culinary Wanderer*." Harper waited for her mother to recognize the name. "He travels all over the world, eating local cuisine and bringing attention to the history or current troubles of the places where he films."

"I don't watch much television. It's too depressing."

Harper didn't bother arguing. Penelope lived in a snug bubble. She played golf in the morning and then lunched with friends. After a few hours spent shopping, the remainder of her day was taken up by something cultural or philanthropic. The only interruption to her schedule happened when she traveled to the Hamptons to visit her mother or decided a room of her condo needed updating.

"His show is very popular."

"I'm sure you know what you're doing," Penelope replied, her tone indicating that she'd dismissed a subject that no longer interested her. "How soon can you get me the money I need?"

"I'll call the bank and have them wire the funds as soon as you tell me who is blackmailing you and why."

"I'm your mother," Penelope huffed. "Don't you dare barter with me."

Before Harper could argue, Mary appeared in the doorway. "Your grandfather is on line one and Carlo called to say Chef Cole wants to talk to you as soon as you're available." Mary placed a wealth of emphasis on that last part.

She needed to do some damage control. "Tell him I'll be down as soon as I'm done talking to Grandfather. Maybe ten or fifteen minutes."

Penelope clutched her daughter's arm as Harper began to rise. "You can't say anything to Henry."

"Why don't we sort this business out over dinner later," she suggested, attempting to pacify her mother. "I need to know more details before we proceed."

"But you are going to help me," Penelope stated, anxiety shadowing her determined tone.

"Of course." Harper's gaze skittered away from the relief in her mother's eyes and fell on her assistant.

Mary had been waiting patiently through their exchange.

Seeing she'd regained Harper's attention, she switched on her headset and spoke to the caller. "She's on her way to the phone now. Okay, I'll let her know. Your grandfather has had to take another call. He'll catch up with you at four our time."

"Thank you, Mary." Harper turned to her mother. "I have some business to take care of. It shouldn't take more than twenty minutes."

Penelope glanced at her watch. "I have a manicure appointment in half an hour."

It made perfect sense to Harper that her mother would schedule a beauty treatment in the midst of a personal crisis. No matter how bad things got, she never neglected her appearance.

"Mary will get you settled in a suite. I'll order dinner to be served there at seven. We can talk then."

Ashton lounged in the Fontaine Ciel's executive conference room, tapping his fingers against the tabletop in a rhythm that called to him from the past. He had his back to the large monitor set on the wall opposite the door that led to the hall. The network suits in New York had not yet figured out the connection was live and he was gaining some useful insights into their thought processes.

He'd been in negotiations for a brand-new television series for almost five months now. The Lifestyle Network wanted him to star in a culinary show that "showcased his talent." Or at least that was the way his manager, Vince, had pitched it. Ashton agreed that it was a solid career move. Something he'd been working toward these past eight years.

It would allow him to live permanently in New York City. He'd never again have to travel under the most uncomfortable conditions to places that no one in their right mind wanted to live.

Too bad he loved all those miserable out-of-the-way places he visited. Nor was Lifestyle Network's demand that he quit *The Culinary Wanderer* if they gave him his new show sitting well with Ashton. With the sort of taping schedule he had with the travel show, there was no reason why he couldn't do both. He'd given six years to Phillips Consolidated Networks and *The Culinary Wanderer*. The show remained vital and continued to do well in the ratings. Giving it up made no sense. And then there was all the aid that the places he visited received as a result of the show.

He hadn't set out to do a culinary series that highlighted socioeconomic and political issues around the world. He'd started out romping around the globe doing a six-part series featuring out of the way culinary adventures for the network's travel channel. At some point toward the end of the first season, he'd started to see the potential of shining the light of television on some of the places regular travelers would never go. But it wasn't until the first segments aired that he realized he was raising social awareness.

The series' high ratings caught the network executives' attention. They liked what they saw and wanted to work with him again so Ashton pitched them a show focused as much on the problems faced by the locals as it was about the regional cuisine. Six months later, *The Culinary Wanderer* was born.

By the end of the first season, his viewership had increased threefold. Inspired by the flood of emails from viewers asking how they could help, the network partnered with a world help organization to bring aid to the areas hit hardest by war and poverty. It was somewhat surreal to discover he did more good with his half-hour television series than his parents did in a year with their missionary work. And it was sad to realize no matter how much he did, they would never approve of his methods.

Still, money had been raised. People had been fed and given medicine. Sources of fresh water had been brought to villages that needed it. But no matter how much Ashton accomplished there was always another town ravaged by unrest or burdened by poverty. His gut told him he shouldn't walk away from all those who still needed help. Yet wasn't it this exact sort of arrogance—that he was somehow special and necessary for others' salvation—that made him so angry with his father?

"Chef Croft, are you ready to begin?"

Ashton swiveled around and gave the assembled group an easy smile. "Whenever you are, gentlemen."

He could see that his manager was on the call from his L.A. office. Vince's expression gave away none of the concern he'd voiced to Ashton late last night, but he wasn't looking as relaxed as usual. This show would take Ashton from celebrity chef to household name. From there the possibilities were endless.

"Chef Croft," began Steven Bell, a midlevel executive who'd been acting as the group's mouthpiece these past several months. He was the third in a line of conservatively dressed, middle-aged men with a talent for pointing out problems and little else. "We have slotted the new show to begin the end of February and would like to start taping in three weeks. Is that a problem?"

"Not at all."

Several of the men exchanged glances, and Ashton picked up on it. If he'd learned anything in the past several months, he'd discovered the path to superstardom wasn't a smooth one.

"We've been told your restaurant in the Fontaine hotel is behind schedule," said the man Ashton thought of as Executive Orange because whatever spray tan he used gave his skin a sunset glow.

"Untrue. It's set to open in two weeks."

"And your expectation is that you'll have it running smoothly immediately?"

Ashton knew what was going on. Vince had warned him that since Ashton was unwilling to give in on the matter of quitting *The Culinary Wanderer* they were looking at other chefs in an effort to force his hand.

"I will be leaving my kitchen in good hands. I offered Chef Dillon Cole the head chef position." He left out the fact that Cole hadn't agreed to take the job.

"He's out of Chicago, correct?"

Unsure which of the six executives had spoken, Ashton nodded. "A talented chef." Which was perfectly true, despite his earlier criticism. Ashton just wasn't sure he was the right man for Batouri, but he was running out of time and options. If he wanted to host the new show, he needed to be available.

"We'd like you to come to New York next week and spend a couple days working with our producers. We feel you should be on the set and run through a couple versions of the show to get some film that we could run past a couple of our current hosts for their input."

"What days did you have in mind?"

"Wednesday and Thursday. We could schedule something in the afternoon, say around two?"

Harper was going to filet him when she caught wind of this impromptu trip. "I'll be there."

"We're looking forward to seeing you."

After a few more niceties and good luck wishes for his restaurant opening, the New York executives signed off. When it was just Ashton and Vince still on the call, the manager let his true feelings show.

"Those bastards are not making this easy, are they?"

"Did you really expect them to?" Ashton countered. "This isn't a travel network with a couple hundred thousand viewers. This channel draws over a million viewers for some of its least popular primetime shows."

"What I expected is for them to be falling all over themselves to bring you in. They're looking to give their lineup more sex appeal. While the numbers have been slipping for cooking shows lately, home improvement segments are on the rise."

"Any idea why?"

"If you listen to my wife and daughter, it's all due to the hunky carpenters they've been hiring."

Ashton grinned. "So you're saying they aren't as interested in my culinary expertise as my impressive physique?"

"How does that make you feel?"

"Like we should be negotiating for more money."

"Maybe I should suggest you do the episodes shirtless."

"Don't give them any ideas." Ashton grimaced. "They'll probably turn it into a bit. Stay tuned for the next segment when Chef Croft will burn off his shirt."

"Well, you'd better get that restaurant of yours open in Vegas or you won't have to worry about what they want you to wear."

"Have you heard from the guys over at Phillips about the proposals I made regarding next season's location?"

In addition to negotiating with the Lifestyle Network, he was in talks with Phillips Consolidated Networks for his seventh season of *The Culinary Wanderer*. They were pushing him to film next season in Africa. They'd reasoned that since he was South African, he would enjoy returning to the land of his birth. The exact opposite was true, but since he'd created an elaborate backstory that had nothing to do with his true history, he couldn't provide an excuse strong enough to dissuade them.

"They rejected England immediately. Apparently your best ratings come when you are off the beaten track. The Indonesian stuff has been a huge hit with everyone who's seen it."

"What about South America? I could get six or seven episodes out of Brazil alone."

"They said they'd consider it for next year." Vince rolled a pen between his palms. "I think if you want to keep doing the show, it's going to have to be Africa. Of course, that's dependent on whether Lifestyle Network gives up on getting an exclusive on you."

Frustration with the producers of *The Culinary Wanderer* had led him to talk to Lifestyle Network. He wanted to grow his career in a big way and the new show could do that. Becoming a household name would open a lot of doors. But it wasn't where his heart lay. He'd never stop craving new adventures in exotic locations. It's why he intended to find a way to do both. Being forced to choose between his passion and his ambition wasn't an option.

"I really don't want to go to Africa."

"Come on. How bad can it be? You still have family there, don't you?"

"Sure." In fact, he had no idea if his parents were still alive. He hadn't spoken to them since he left home at fifteen. A lot of bad things could happen in twenty years, especially in the sort of places his parents took their missionary work.

He heard the door open behind him and noticed the change in Vince's demeanor. His manager sat forward in his desk chair and ran his fingers through his short sandy-blond hair. Glancing over his shoulder, Ashton noticed Harper had entered the room. She didn't look happy.

"Gotta go, Vince. Keep in touch." He ended the network connection and the monitor in the room went blank. "Thanks for letting me borrow your equipment. This is some nice stuff."

"Chef Cole tells me he's not going to be our head chef."

"I offered him the job just like you wanted."

"I wanted you to hire him."

"He turned me down." Ashton pushed his chair back from the conference table and stood up.

"So, now what?"

"You have me."

"I need someone permanent. How long before you take off again?"

Next week, but in her current state of displeasure, he wasn't going to mention that.

"Not to worry. I have someone I trust who I've been training. He arrives tomorrow."

"Who is it?"

"I met Dae Tan a few months ago. Helped him out of a jam."

"What sort of a jam?" Her skepticism came through loud and clear.

"He was arrested for something he didn't do."

"You're sure he was innocent."

"Absolutely. After that, things got a little hot for him. He's been traveling with me and I've been training him."

"Why didn't he come with you today?"

"He wanted to see L.A. He has this thing about movie stars."

Harper regarded him with suspicion. "Where has he worked? Is he capable of handling the pressure of a restaurant like Batouri?"

"It'll be fine. The kid's got talent."

"Kid?" She echoed his description and her irritation grew. "How old is he?"

"Twenty-five. Twenty-six."

"You can't be serious." Harper advanced on him. "You've passed on chefs with twenty-five *years* of experience and now you're telling me you want to hire someone who's been in the field a couple years."

"Months," Ashton corrected. "He only had the most rudimentary skills when I met him."

Harper's eyes closed while she sucked in a deep breath and let it out. When she opened them again, she looked no calmer. "You're crazy if you think I'll go for this."

"You really don't have a choice."

"We'll see about that." Harper folded her arms across her chest. "You forget we have a contract." Her tone indicated he'd stretched her goodwill as far as it would go.

"I have a great deal riding on this restaurant, as well," he reminded her.

"Then act like it."

The trouble was, he had a great deal riding on every iron he had in the fire. He was determined to leave his mark on the world and that meant going big. Would it have been smarter to not stick his neck out? Sure. He could have played it safe, kept going with the same shows he'd had success with these past eight years, but Ashton liked the rush of conquering new territory, seeing what lay beyond the horizon.

Harper continued, "Go convince Cole to take the job at Batouri."

"I thought you said he'd gone to the airport."

"I caught him before he left the hotel and convinced him to fly to Chicago tomorrow. You have reservations next door at Fontaine Chic's award-winning steakhouse at seven. You might as well sample the competition. Perhaps you will both dislike the food and find some common ground to build a relationship on."

"And our evening together?"

She shot him a cool smile. "When Cole takes the job, I'll block out two hours for you."

"Make it three and you have a deal."

Three

With the Chef Cole problem handled for the time being and her mother safely ensconced in the day spa, Harper was able to steal a few minutes to herself to take stock of the day. Thank heavens they weren't all like this.

Unable to imagine what her mother had done to open herself up to blackmail, Harper paced her hotel, trying to find comfort in achievement. The ceilings throughout had been painted to represent different aspects of the sky her hotel was named for. In the lobby, it was a pale midday blue dotted with clouds. Lighting changed from dawn to dusk to match what was happening outside. The casino ceiling was a midnight indigo sparkling with thousands of pinpoint lights configured like the star patterns above Las Vegas.

It was a simple concept, beautifully rendered. She was proud of all she'd accomplished. But today, there was no joy to be found in surveying her domain. Harper glanced at her watch. Two hours to kill. With her ability to concentrate shot and no meetings or crisis pending, she considered returning to her suite and running on her treadmill. Or she could go talk to Scarlett.

Five years ago when her grandfather had come to her with news that she had two half sisters, she'd been angry, miserable and excited. She'd been eleven when she'd first learned her father regularly cheated on his wife, but until five years ago, she'd had no idea his extramarital wandering had messed up more lives than just hers and her mother's.

A quick walk through the skyways that connected the three Fontaine hotels brought Harper to Fontaine Richesse, Scarlett's hotel. She sought out her sister in the casino. Spotting Scarlett was easy. She radiated sex appeal and charisma in her emerald-green flapper costume, her long brown hair tucked beneath a twenties-style, shingle bob wig with bangs.

The rest of the casino staff was dressed like something out of a movie from the forties and fifties: men in elegant tuxedos and suits or military uniforms from the Second World War, women in evening gowns or stylish dresses.

Harper had thought the whole idea of a Golden Age of Hollywood night was crazy. But she'd underestimated her sister's brilliance. The casino was packed. Many of those playing the machines or lining the tables were also dressed in costume. There were prizes awarded for best outfit, and casino cash was given to anyone who guessed what particular movie the dealers or waitresses were dressed from.

Scarlett wore a delighted grin as the man who'd approached her guessed her costume.

"Cyd Charrise, *Singin' In The Rain?*"

"That's right." She handed him a card he could trade in for money to gamble with. As he walked off, she spotted Harper. "What a surprise."

"You look amazing," Harper said, admiring the dress and matching green satin pumps. "Is it new?"

"First time I've worn it." She struck a pose. "I think Laurie outdid herself." Scarlett had been friends with the

Hollywood costume designer for years and used her for every costume in the casino.

"I would agree."

When she'd first met Scarlett, Harper hadn't given the former child actress much credit. She couldn't imagine what her grandfather had been thinking when he'd concocted the contest between his three granddaughters. What could someone with Scarlett's background know about running a multibillion-dollar hotel much less a corporation the size of Fontaine Hotels and Resorts? Five years later, Harper was a huge fan of Scarlett's creativity and authenticity. She knew exactly who she was and had played directly to her strengths.

"Do you have time for a drink?" Harper asked, instantly seeing her request had startled Scarlett.

Harper was the family workaholic. Rarely did she sit down in the evenings when the casino was busiest, much less take time out to eat or drink.

"For you, always." They found a table in a quiet corner of the lobby bar. Scarlett ordered two glasses of cabernet and made small talk until the drinks arrived. "What's wrong?" she asked as soon as Harper had taken a sip of wine.

"What makes you think…?" She could see Scarlett wasn't fooled. "I don't want you to assume that I'm only here because I needed help."

"I don't care why you're here." Scarlett gave her a lopsided smile. "And I'm glad Violet is out of town with JT. Otherwise, I know you'd have gone to her first."

"That's unfair." But probably true. As much as Harper loved her half sister, she wasn't always comfortable with Scarlett.

In so many ways, they were opposites. Scarlett was gorgeous, flamboyant and utterly fearless when it came to her relationships. Hadn't she tackled Logan Wolfe and turned the tetchy security expert into a big purring lion?

She'd managed to do the same thing with Harper. Wariness had become loyalty, something Harper gave rarely and not without reservation. But Scarlett had won her over for the most part.

"Okay, there is something wrong." Harper paused, knowing Scarlett deserved more. "But you aren't right about how I'd go to Violet instead of you. If she was here, I'd have come to both of you with this."

"Must be serious." Scarlett's lips curved into a wicked smile. "Do you need some advice about Ashton Croft? I heard he's back in town."

"Nothing like that."

"I suggest you sleep with him."

"What?" Harper cursed the sudden heat in her cheeks. "I'm not going to sleep with him. Our relationship is strictly professional."

"You should reconsider that. I know you have a thing for him. And he looks like he'd be a riot in bed."

Harper needed Scarlett to get off that particular subject. "My mother is being blackmailed."

All mischief went out of Scarlett. She paled. "Blackmailed? Why?"

"I don't know. She won't tell me."

"Does she know who is doing it?"

Harper shook her head. "It's all so crazy. My mother. The perfect Penelope Fontaine. I can't imagine her doing anything wrong much less anything scandalous enough to invite blackmail."

"How did you find out?"

"She came here needing to borrow money."

"How much?"

"Three hundred and fifty thousand."

Scarlett gasped. "That's a lot."

"I keep wondering what she's done. It must be something truly awful for them to be asking that much."

"From what you've told me," Scarlett began, "your

mother isn't great at considering the value of something before she spends. Is she sure what happened is worth that much money?"

"It's hard to say with my mother. She's so big on keeping her reputation unsullied, it might be something as simple as a bump and run." But Harper couldn't picture her mother having a minor accident much less fleeing the scene of one.

"Could she have cheated on her taxes?"

"Impossible. Grandfather handles all her finances." Penelope's lack of financial smarts was what had caused Grandfather to put her on an allowance and hire a money manager to pay the bills.

"I don't suppose she wants to call the police." Scarlett framed the question as if she already knew the answer.

"She won't do that," Harper said. "The blackmailer will make her secret public."

"Do you need help coming up with the cash? I have some money set aside."

Her sister's offer came so fast Harper doubted Scarlett considered the magnitude of the gesture. She was humbled by her sister's affection. "Thanks, but I didn't come here for that."

"Then why?"

"I thought talking with you would put me in a calmer frame of mind before I have dinner with my mother."

"She's here?"

"Showed up this afternoon out of the blue."

Harper had never spoken directly about how she and Penelope got along, but both her sisters knew that Harper's mother had left her daughter behind in New York City and moved to Florida. It wasn't a stretch to deduce that things between mother and daughter weren't good. But if anyone understood that family could produce the most complicated relationships, it would be Harper and Scarlett.

"Why don't I talk with Logan," Scarlett suggested. "Maybe there's something he or Lucas can do."

"I don't know if anyone can help at this point."

"Are you kidding? Logan and his brother are security experts. They should be able to figure out who's blackmailing your mom without breaking a sweat. If not before the blackmail is paid, then I know they can track where the money goes."

Harper was suddenly feeling a whole lot better. Impulsively, she hugged Scarlett. "I don't know what I would do without you and Violet."

"I'm glad to hear you say that. I wasn't always sure you liked having us in your life."

Scarlett's admission twisted Harper's stomach into knots of regret. "I'm sorry I've made you feel that way. In the beginning it wasn't easy embracing you as sisters. I'd been alone my whole life and hadn't exactly been smothered with love by my parents. I didn't really understand what it meant to be family."

"I hope that's changed."

"It has. You and Violet are the most important people in my life along with Grandfather." Seeing the tears that filled Scarlett's beautiful green eyes, Harper wished she'd made this confession long ago. "I'm sorry if I made it seem otherwise. I've been so focused on getting Fontaine Ciel built and running that I haven't been a very good sister."

Scarlett waved the apology away and dabbed at her eyes with a napkin. Delight filled her voice as she said, "You didn't need to say anything. We knew how you felt."

Harper made a resolution to be more open with her sisters going forward. It wouldn't be easy. She'd spent her whole life bottling up her feelings. Her mother wasn't demonstrative and her father's rare appearances in her life hadn't been filled with warm moments. In school she'd been a leader and her habit of ruling by persuasion and occasional ruthlessness hadn't won her the love of the majority of her classmates. But it hadn't mattered as long as they followed her. Or so she'd told herself.

"Let me call Logan and see what he suggests we do."

"I'm sure he's not going to want you to do anything," Harper said with a faint smile.

"Since when has that stopped me?"

Scarlett had given her fiancé a lot to worry about after inheriting some files from Tiberius Stone, Violet's surrogate father. The casino owner had been murdered by a local councilman who'd been embezzling campaign contributions. Tiberius had accumulated a storage unit full of people's secrets including his brother-in-law, a man who'd stolen the identity of Preston Rhodes, a wealthy orphan from California. Violet had gone to Miami intent on bringing him to justice in order to help her husband take back his family's company.

"It's rolling to voice mail," Scarlett said. After leaving Logan a brief summary of the situation, she hung up. "It won't take him long to call me back. Do you want to wait?"

About to say yes, Harper suddenly remembered she still had Ashton's *go* bag. "Can't. I have to see a man about a bag."

Scarlett cocked her head in puzzlement, but nodded. "As soon as I hear from Logan, I'll call you. In the meantime, can you stall your mother?"

"I can try."

Leaving Scarlett, Harper made her way back to the Fontaine Ciel's executive floor. Mary had gone for the day, locking Harper's office before she left. Harper half expected Ashton to have persuaded the personal assistant to give him his bag, but to her surprise, either Mary had resisted the celebrity chef's charm or Ashton had stuck to his part of the bargain.

Either way, she grabbed the bag and shot a quick text to let him know the luggage would be waiting for him at Batouri. But when she got there, she was surprised to find Ashton sitting at the corner table where his bag had sat earlier.

* * *

When the door to the restaurant opened, Ashton was nursing a tumbler of ten-year-old Scotch. It was his third. The first two had gone down fast and smooth. He didn't think he should continue at that pace or his dinner with Cole might not go the way Harper wanted.

That she spotted him so fast made him smile. She felt it, too. This irresistible pull between them. How had he ignored it until now? Oh, she was good at hiding it. And he hadn't exactly given her any reason to feel more than irritation toward him. He wanted to strip her layers of professionalism away and get to the firecracker below. How hot would the fire burn? And for how long? With fireworks, the thrill was in those seconds of exhilarating danger. The breathtaking waterfall of light. The big boom that lingered in the chest even after the sound faded.

Still, it might be worth sacrificing her goodwill to experience the rush.

"What brings you here?" He sipped the Scotch, felt the burn in his chest.

"I'm returning your *go* bag."

He'd been so focused on Harper he hadn't even noticed that she was towing his bag along.

You're slipping.

In the places he traveled, being distracted for even a moment could be trouble.

"The deal isn't done with Cole yet," he reminded her. "Are you sure you don't want to keep it hostage for a bit longer?" Maybe take it back to her suite. "I could pick it up later."

She parked the bag beside the booth. "I've lost my taste for blackmail in the past few hours." Her gaze flicked to the glass and then to his mouth.

His heart tapped unsteadily against his ribs. "Anything you'd like to talk about?"

"No."

"Are you sure?"

Was it the alcohol that was making him light-headed or the way she was staring at him as if she wondered what he'd taste like? She reached for his glass, and he figured she was going to chastise him for drinking up the restaurant's stock. Instead, she lifted the tumbler to her lips and tossed back the last ounce of Scotch. He expected her to come up coughing as the strong liquor hit her throat. Instead, she licked her lips and smiled, her eyes thoughtful and distant.

"My grandfather loves Scotch." She set the glass back on the table and turned to go.

"I'm a very good listener." Ashton claimed few virtues. Giving a speaker his full attention was one. But would she trust him to share what was going on?

Harper hesitated before facing him once more. "My mother came into town unexpectedly."

Ashton relaxed, unaware until his lungs started working again that he'd been holding his breath. "I noticed the air between you two wasn't particularly cheerful."

"Do you have a good relationship with your parents?"

He shook his head, the twinge in his gut barely noticeable. "I left home at fifteen and never looked back."

"I've read everything ever written about you and I'm pretty sure that wasn't part of your history."

He knew better than to be flattered. "It's a story for another day. We're talking about you."

Her gaze was steady on his for several seconds. "My mother moved to Florida when I was eleven, leaving me in New York with my father who was rarely home. At the time I hated her for not being around, but as I grew up, I realized that being away from her criticism gave me the freedom to make mistakes and learn from them without being afraid she'd make me feel worse."

"I'm not sure many people would be as unaffected by their mother's abandonment as you are."

Harper gave him a wry smile. "Don't for a second think

I'm unaffected. I'm just realistic. My mother didn't abandon me. She fled a situation she'd didn't like. Penelope isn't someone who stands and fights when she can run away and go shopping." Harper shrugged, but she was far from sounding nonchalant. "Okay, so maybe I'm a little more bothered than I let on."

"It's nice to hear you admit that."

"Why?"

"Because I like you and I haven't been able to figure out why."

"You like me?" Her breathless laugh wasn't the reaction he'd expected.

"Very much," he admitted, more than a little disturbed by the way her delighted smile transformed her into a stunning, vivacious woman.

"After the way I've hounded you these past nine months?" She shook her head, and the career woman took over once more. "I think you're just trying to charm me. If this is your way of changing my mind about Chef Cole, you've got it all wrong."

"So suspicious," he taunted. "That's not it at all. I'm starting to come around to your opinion about Cole. As for the way you've acted these past few months, I get it. This hotel is important to you. Batouri will make a statement and depending on how it does, that statement will be good or bad. I'd be a hypocrite to criticize you for doing whatever it took to make sure Batouri is a complete success."

"That's awfully accommodating of you."

Rub me the right way and I can be very accommodating.

But that's the sort of comeback she'd expect. "Does your mother visit you in Las Vegas often?"

"Never. She hates it here."

"Must be important for her to show up then."

"She needs my help. Which is different. She usually

takes her problems to my grandfather because he's a man and taking care of women is what men do."

"That sounds very traditional minded."

"It goes against everything I believe in. I'm a modern career girl." A trace of self-mockery put a lilt in her voice. "She disapproves of my choices. Thinks I should have married a tycoon like my grandfather and dazzled New York society on his arm."

"That seems like a waste of your intelligence and drive."

"It's hard being a disappointment."

"I agree." This they shared. No matter how much either of them accomplished, they weren't living up to their parents' perception of success. "It spoils what you've achieved, doesn't it."

She looked surprised by his insight. Her gaze became keen as it rested on him. "It does."

He lifted the bottle of Scotch. "Do you want another drink?" He was dying to watch her swallow another glass. And then lick her lips again. There'd been something so decadent, so wickedly un-Harper-like about the deed.

"I should get back to work."

"See you tomorrow night."

"Text me when Chef Cole agrees to come work for you." She started to leave, but then paused. "Thanks for listening."

He suspected voicing her gratitude hadn't come easily. "Anytime. You know where to find me."

Shaking her head in exasperation, Harper spun away and headed toward the exit, her stride purposeful. Whatever sharing she'd done, it was now over. Ashton was left with an increased appreciation for Harper Fontaine.

These past few months he'd assumed her arrogance was a natural byproduct of her family's money and connections, that life was a breeze for her. He'd been as guilty of stereotyping as his critics often were. To be fair, her confidence had always been dent-free.

Now he realized there were a few pinholes in her armor.

And they had more in common than he'd have ever guessed.

Harper pushed lettuce around on her plate, her appetite deadened by the smell of cigarette smoke. The suite would have to be deep cleaned before any guests could be booked in here. Over dinner, her mother had refused to speak about the blackmail. Harper's impatience was growing with each minute that ticked by. She set down her fork. It clattered on the china. The discordant sound startled her mother.

"We have to talk about why you're here."

"I don't want to."

"If you expect me to give you three hundred and fifty thousand dollars, I'm going to need to know why you're being blackmailed."

"I can't tell you."

"Did you kill someone?"

"Don't be an idiot."

"That's a relief," Harper muttered. She left the table, needing activity to think. As she crossed the room, a dozen ideas sprang into her mind. She picked the most likely one and turned to confront her mother. "You stole something."

"I'm not a thief." Penelope stubbed out her cigarette and reached for another, but Harper beat her to the package.

"No more smoking."

Her mother glared at her. "You are trying to provoke me into telling you something you're not ready to hear."

Why not? Harper mused. Her mother had been aggravating her for years. "I'm trying to figure out what could be worth three hundred and fifty thousand dollars."

"Actually it's a million."

"A mill…?" Harper crushed the cigarette package in her fist.

Penelope pouted. "It's a small price to pay compared to the consequences."

"What sort of consequences?"

"Life or death."

Now her mother had gone too far. "This is serious, Mother. You need to talk to Grandfather."

"I can't. He'd demand to know why I was being black-mailed. I can't tell him."

"Give me some idea what the blackmail is or I'm going to call him."

Penelope shot her daughter a wounded look. "There are some indelicate photos that if they got out would be very damaging."

Unsure how her conservative mother defined indelicate, Harper sought clarification. "Surely it can't be that bad."

"It could ruin us."

Us?

For a second Harper wasn't sure whom her mother was referring to. Penelope certainly hadn't worried about her daughter's welfare when she ran off to Florida.

"Who is 'us'?" she questioned, her voice scarcely audible.

Her mother looked startled. "Why you and I, of course."

Harper knelt beside Penelope. Taking her mother's hands, surprised by the icy chill in her fingers, Harper squeezed just hard enough to capture Penelope's full attention.

"If this involves me, you need to tell me what is going on."

"I had an affair," Penelope whispered, unable to maintain eye contact with Harper. Her mother was something other than mortified. She was afraid. "If that came out—" She broke off and shook her head.

Was something besides her mother's reputation at stake? "Who was it?"

"I met him at an exhibition of wildlife photography in London. His work was being honored." She released an impassioned sigh. "His photos were amazing."

"You had an affair with a photographer." Harper didn't know what to think. She had little trouble imaging her mother dallying with a duke or an Italian prince while in London, but a wildlife photographer?

"He was exciting and handsome and I couldn't get enough of his stories of Africa. He actually lived in the bush for ten months to get one particular shot of a group of lions."

Harper couldn't stop herself from drawing a parallel between her fascination with Ashton's adventures and her mother having an affair with someone who lived dangerously. Harper winced away from the comparison, dismayed to think she was more like her mother than she'd ever imagined.

"When did you have this affair?"

"Your father was out of the country a great deal."

"Before you split." Is that what had caused her mother to go to Florida? Had she been banished for being unfaithful? That seemed awfully unfair considering her husband's rampant infidelities. "Did Daddy know?"

"Not at first. I was very discreet. But in the end he figured it out."

"Why did you and father stay married when that's obviously not what either of you wanted?"

"What makes you think either of us wanted a divorce? Your father married me to cement a deal for Henry to buy my family's hotels. It was never a love match. I received security in exchange for ignoring all his affairs. It wasn't as if he intended to marry any of those women he slept with." Penelope sipped at her wine. "As for my brief indiscretion—" her mother offered an indifferent shrug "—I was out of the country and I knew I'd never see him again."

Yet thirty years later keeping the affair from being revealed was worth a million dollars. Was it just her mother's overdeveloped sense of propriety at work or was there something more going on?

"How brief an indiscretion was it?" Curiosity overpowered Harper as she tried to imagine her mother as young, impulsive and happy. All three were a stretch.

Penelope shot her a repressive frown. "What does it matter?"

How could her mother not understand how fascinating Harper found all this? Harper's whole life she'd had this image of her mother as the victim of Ross Fontaine's adulterous wandering. Suffering because her pride or a sense of honor kept her from divorcing the man who made her miserable.

"I'm just having a hard time picturing you..." Harper couldn't think of a way to say what was on her mind without it sounding like an insult.

"Engaging in a torrid affair?" Penelope spat out the words as if they tasted bad.

"I was going to say happy."

The diamond on Penelope's left hand sent out spikes of color as she waved away Harper's explanation. "Happy is overrated."

Was it? Harper considered her own life. Was she happy? Content maybe. Unless she compared herself to Violet and Scarlett and then she looked positively miserable. Being in love had certainly given her sisters a glow.

But it wasn't just being in love, for often love didn't last in a relationship. It was the fact that they'd found the other half of themselves. It wasn't something Harper had imagined for herself. Her ideal life involved a large executive office in Fontaine's New York City headquarters, rising profits, a cover article in *Forbes*. She didn't think in terms of a private life. She couldn't imagine having the energy to navigate the unpredictable waters of a serious relationship.

Once again her thoughts drifted to Ashton Croft and the awareness that spiked through her every time they occupied the same room. Regret rubbed at her. As much as he irritated her as a businessman, she was wildly attracted to the adventurous chef. If her responsibilities didn't weigh her down, she wouldn't hesitate to take those dimples of his for a spin.

"I don't see anything about this situation worth smiling over," Harper's mother stated, her voice sharp and impatient.

Harper pushed Ashton out of her mind and resumed her mask of professionalism. "You're right. There isn't."

"How soon can I get the money?"

"First thing tomorrow. What are we supposed to do? Gather the cash in a briefcase and drop it off at the bus station?"

Harper was struck with untimely amusement by the idea of her mother setting one Manolo-clad toe in such a place. But the urge to laugh vanished abruptly as she recalled Ashton's assessing gaze earlier. In all likelihood he had the same opinion about her. Worse, he'd be right. She'd never been to a bus station or ridden a bus. She'd spent her whole childhood in New York City and had only used the subway once.

"Don't be ridiculous," her mother said. "The money is to be wired. I've been given an account."

"That's safer." And she'd bet Scarlett's fiancé had a team of computer experts that could track the money to its final destination. "Give me the account number and I'll take care of everything."

Four

"Wow, boss." Dae's white grin split his tanned face as he toured Batouri's kitchen. "Nice place you got here."

The former Bali surfing instructor gazed around in admiration, taking in the pristine appliances and immaculate counters. Ashton had picked Dae up at the airport half an hour earlier and had intended to take him straight to the apartment he'd rented, but Dae had wanted to see the kitchen first. Ashton understood. He'd been discussing the project with the young Balinese man for the past four months. Naturally, he was curious.

"Glad you like it. You sure this is where you want to be? You have no idea what Chef Cole is going to be like to work with." Ashton had smoothed things over with the Chicago chef and persuaded him to accept the job at Batouri.

"Can't be worse than you."

Ashton ignored the taunt. "He'll probably start you at the bottom. I'm not sure that's the best use of your talents. I could find you something in one of my New York or London restaurants."

Dae shook his head. "I like Vegas. It's happening."

After marking the first twenty-five years of his life by island time, Dae was looking for a little excitement. Ashton understood. Hadn't he gotten out of Africa at twenty for the exact same reason?

"Just don't lose your shirt gambling."

"No worries." Dae tugged at the tails of his bright tropical shirt. "No one would give me a nickel for this thing."

"That's not what I meant," Ashton began, before seeing that his protégé was pulling his leg. "That dumb island boy stuff isn't going to get you too far."

Dae winked. "It got me here and that's pretty far."

With a rueful grin, Ashton stopped playing wise old guy. The role didn't suit him. Usually he was the one on the receiving end of advice, not the other way around. It was just that most of the time in Dae's company, the ten-year age difference seemed more like twenty.

Ever since he'd brought the young Indonesian kid under his wing, Ashton had felt responsible for him. Owner of four restaurants with over a hundred staff, he had a lot of people depending on him. But that was business. With Dae it was personal.

A chance to pay forward against a debt he could never repay.

"I found you a place to stay not far from here. It's on the bus line."

"You know I appreciate all you've done for me."

"Someone helped me out once. It changed my life." Saved it was more like it. And Dae was far more deserving of help than Ashton had ever been. "The best way to repay me is to succeed."

"You know I will."

That was the great thing about Dae. He had a limitless reserve of optimism. Even when his situation had been truly bad in Bali, he'd just grinned and said that things would get better. And they had because Ashton had traded cooking lessons for surfing lessons and discovered the kid had a natural aptitude and a fantastic palate.

"Shall we go check out your new apartment?" Ashton gestured toward the exit.

"Lead the way. How are things going with the new show?" Dae asked as Ashton got behind the wheel of the SUV he'd rented and started the engine.

"I'm not sure. They're still demanding I give up *The Culinary Wanderer*."

"You gonna?"

"The producers haven't stopped pushing Africa for next year and you know how I feel about it."

"Maybe you should forget about them. Do the show in New York."

Sound advice. Vince had been urging him in the same direction. Even his own brain was telling him to dump the travel show and move on to bigger and better things. And with the Phillips producers digging in their heels about doing next year's show in Africa, there didn't seem to be any good reason to sign a new contract.

So why was he having trouble letting go?

"That's probably what's going to end up happening," Ashton said. "I'll know more next week when I go meet with them. They want me to make a pilot for some people to look at."

"What are you going to do?"

"I have a few ideas."

None of which felt quite right. When they'd first approached him, Ashton had known exactly what he wanted to do. But as the negotiations lengthened, the more he learned about their concept for the show, the less confident he was that it was the sort of thing he wanted to do. And yet, the opportunity to take his career to the next level was a temptation he couldn't reject out of hand.

Once he'd settled Dae in his new apartment, Ashton

returned to the hotel. Dae's questions had prodded him into action.

He was beginning to wonder if they would ever see eye to eye on this project and what would happen if they didn't. After his last round of recipes had been rejected by the producers as too exotic, Ashton was finding it hard to come up with anything that excited him. Was it supposed to be this hard? Ashton didn't remember ever having to struggle like this to make anything happen in his career. Sure, he'd worked hard. Pushed himself to the limits of his energy and beyond. During his years filming *The Culinary Wanderer,* he'd been chilled to the bone, taken shelter from a tropical storm in a shallow cave, broken his arm, sprained his knee and been grazed by a ricocheting bullet. In the days before he'd landed his first television show, he'd worked for arrogant chefs who'd made his life hell but hadn't cared because it had been all about the food.

This was different. The executives of Lifestyle Network weren't thinking about good food or interesting stories— they wanted big numbers, and to them that meant doing something everyone could relate to. Ashton didn't think that would ever play to his strengths. Unless Vince was right and they were just hiring him to up their beefcake quotient.

The thought both amused and horrified him.

Ashton pushed aside the notes he'd been scribbling for the show and went to work on the more immediate problem. Figuring out Batouri's menu. Harper would expect culinary perfection and a cohesive plan for how that would happen. Impressing her should have been secondary in his thoughts. But he liked what happened when she dropped her guard and that only happened when he surprised her.

Unfortunately, an hour after sitting down with his thick notebook filled with recipes he'd gathered over the years, inspiration still eluded him. He was on the verge of picking ten at random when he heard the clink of china and looked up as Harper slid into the booth opposite him.

When Harper first entered the restaurant and spotted Ashton at the corner table he seemed to prefer, she realized they were both stuck in a rut. Him, sitting in the dim restaurant brooding. Her, tracking him down like some infatuated groupie. Which she was. But her reasons for coming here were a little more complicated than simple hero worship.

Last night, she'd left the restaurant feeling calmer and more grounded than when she'd arrived. Perhaps he wasn't the most reliable or altruistic man she'd ever met, but his brand of roguish charm had provided a much-needed distraction.

Today he was bent over a notebook, a cup of coffee at his elbow. It was the first time she'd ever seen him this utterly focused on his work. Usually he was a whirling dervish of energy. Flamboyant and passionate while interviewing chefs, directing staff in the bright stainless-steel kitchen or conveying his vision for the decor, gesturing broadly to emphasize whatever point he was trying to make.

As she studied him, some of her anxiety faded. Even sitting still, his body hummed with energy. Yet last night, he'd been an oasis of peace in her otherwise chaotic day. The experience had surprised her. She'd stayed to chat with him, looking to be distracted for a little while. With Scarlett's teasing still occupying her thoughts, was it any wonder she'd been contemplating what being with him would be like?

She'd assumed all he could offer her would be mind-blowing sex with no strings. Her perception had changed when he shared that he'd left home at fifteen and never looked back. She was certain this was something few knew. Why had he given her a glimpse of the man behind the celebrity? He was more complicated than she'd imagined and that spurred her fascination with him to new heights.

It also made tumbling into bed with him a lot riskier than she'd first thought.

Her head told her to turn around and walk out the door. Life had become complicated enough without falling for Ashton Croft. But curiosity drove her forward. She simply had to know what he was working on.

Grabbing a cup from the wait station as she passed, she slid into the booth beside Ashton. He'd been lost in thought, but looked up as the cushion shifted with her weight. Without questioning her reason for joining him, he took her cup and filled it with coffee from the stainless-steel airpot.

"Checking up on me?"

"Do I need to?"

"Probably." He flipped through the notebook, displaying pages filled with his bold handwriting. "I'm going a dozen different directions."

"I never expected you to second-guess yourself." She pulled his notebook toward her. "I always picture you jumping off the cliff without checking to see if there's a safer way down."

"Maybe you're rubbing off on me a little."

His claim made her grin. "Then my work here is done."

"Not even close. You need to help me finalize my menu."

"Me?"

"For someone who doesn't eat, you have one of the best palates I've ever known."

"I eat," she protested. "I just make sure it's healthy. And I exercise a lot. Running helps me think."

"If you ask me, you need to spend less time in your head."

"I don't remember asking you." Her mild tone kept harshness out of the retort. "But that hasn't stopped you from offering your opinion in the past."

"Stop trying to provoke me and pick a dish that appeals to you."

Resisting a grin, Harper focused on Ashton's notebook.

She'd never had a relationship where she felt comfortable being playful. In New York the men she dated were serious types whose pedigrees would satisfy her mother. Ashton didn't fit that mold. And her grandfather's opinion of him was what mattered to her. Henry Fontaine appreciated Ashton's rise from humble beginnings. Her grandfather had built his hotel empire through hard work, too.

After a while, Harper found herself unable to choose a single dish from the recipes he'd jotted down, which only caused her admiration for Ashton to grow. Each dish sounded better than the last. The man was nothing short of brilliant. She saw why he was having trouble settling on his menu. He had enough here for ten restaurants.

"Any one of these would be perfect. It's too bad you can't make them all." She slid the notebook back toward him. "You should do a cookbook. One of the things your television show didn't do was spotlight your talent."

His eyes narrowed as he studied her. "I've missed cooking. It's part of why I'm looking at doing a kitchen-based show for Lifestyle Network."

Harper sighed. Because his other restaurants were critically well received and extremely profitable, she hadn't been able to understand his lack of focus when it came to Batouri. Now she was beginning to realize it was a timing issue. He'd put his television career ahead of the restaurant at every turn. And now he was entertaining the idea of a new project. No wonder he was finding it too difficult to settle down and focus on the mundane details required to make the restaurant successful.

"We've come too far to change things now," Harper began, determined to voice her concerns. "But I have to ask if you're truly committed to making Batouri successful."

"Of course."

When she'd first approached him about the restaurant, she'd hoped they'd form a partnership. Blinded by her admiration for his talent, she hadn't realized that Ashton liked to fly solo.

"It just seems as if your attention isn't one hundred percent focused on this project."

"I'm in negotiations for the next season of my show, but most of that is being handled by my manager. I'm committed to getting the restaurant up and running."

She hoped that was true, but what was going to happen when this new show took off? He already had four other restaurants and *The Culinary Wanderer.* Now a new show?

"Will you have time to do both shows plus manage all your restaurants?"

"I'm not sure I'm going to be doing *The Culinary Wanderer* much longer."

Disappointment raced through her. "You can't stop." What could possibly provide him the same thrill as filming in a country where travel was risky due to political upheaval or in remote locations that few outsiders bothered to visit? Playing it safe wasn't Ashton's first priority. "That show is wonderful."

"I don't want to stop," he told her. "But it's a sticking point in the negotiations for the new show. They want me to be exclusive to the Lifestyle Network."

"Why exclusive?"

"They're planning on promoting the hell out of the new show and the exposure will lead to bigger things."

"And that's what's important to you?" Part of her recognized it was none of her business, but she couldn't get enough of his travel show. She'd seen every episode at least three times. "I thought you loved traveling to out-of-the-way places and meeting new people."

"I do." He rubbed his temple with his palm. "It's just that I'm looking for new challenges and this new show fits the bill."

"You're sure you can't do both?"

"You were just asking me if I was going to have time."

"That was before I realized you were going to stop doing *The Culinary Wanderer*."

"Sorry to disappoint you."

She wished she'd kept quiet. Badgering him with her concerns wasn't constructive. He wasn't a man she could control. In the past nine months she'd learned that lesson all too well.

"It's none of my business. I just love your show."

"Thank you." Ashton put his hand over hers and squeezed gently. "I'll make several dishes I'm on the fence about including on the menu. You offer your opinion and we'll get everything finalized tonight."

Harper knew it was an unnecessary exercise. No matter what she suggested, he would select his menu based on his preferences. But she appreciated his effort to put her mind at ease.

"Sure."

"Come back at eight?"

She slid from the booth. "See you then."

As she exited the restaurant she glanced at her phone. She'd muted it before starting her conversation with Ashton, and now saw that she'd missed six calls and ten emails. Heaving a sigh, she lengthened her stride and headed for her office.

The interlude with Ashton had increased her anxiety rather than calmed her. She caught herself scowling as she rode the elevator to the administrative floor. It was just a television show, she reminded herself, unsure if that was all there was to it. For a half an hour once a week she got to escape the constant pressure of the hotel and travel with Ashton as he learned about elephant conservation in Sri Lanka or braved the Fairy Meadow Road in Pakistan.

The vicarious thrill was a secret she preferred to keep hidden because it didn't sync with the levelheaded, hardworking hotel executive she was 99 percent of the time. Her compulsive desire to protect the secret left her questioning many of the choices she'd made. And she knew nothing good would come of doubting herself.

Ashton crossed his arms over his chest, the white executive chef's jacket pulling tight against his shoulders. He had outdone himself. After Harper had left him that afternoon, he'd benefited from a creative surge that resulted in eight brand new entrées. Each one was something he thought she'd enjoy based on what had caught her attention in his notebook of recipes.

He'd gladly let her preferences define his menu. Batouri wouldn't exist without her. In the past twenty-four hours, as he'd immersed himself in planning, he'd discovered a sense of purpose he hadn't expected. It wasn't in his nature to stop and reflect. Like a shark, he needed to keep swimming in order to stay alive. Or was it to feel alive?

At precisely eight o'clock, Harper entered the kitchen. His pulse jabbed against his throat as he surveyed her. She'd changed into a sleeveless wrap dress made with layers of ethereal blue-gray material.

"What you're wearing reminds me of a fog bank I saw on a motorcycle ride in the highlands of Vietnam last year." He paused, unaccustomed to sharing his thoughts when he wasn't in front of the camera.

She tilted her head, signaling interest. "Tell me about it."

"We had a couple days off from filming so I rented a bike and headed up into the mountains. As you can imagine, the road was narrow and poorly maintained. I'd meet cars and trucks careening around hairpin turns with no guardrails between the road and the sheer cliffs."

"Sounds terrifying."

"It should have been. I'd pass villages where kids ran out into the road. I was chased by dogs." Amid all the craziness he'd felt both exhilarated and completely at peace. "At one point I glanced over my shoulder and down into the valley. A fog hung over the lush green far below."

In those hours he'd not known where he was headed and hadn't cared. The journey was everything. His time in Harper's company was the same. He wanted to live in the present, but she was a woman who needed to know what lay ahead. How far could their relationship develop before she grew frustrated with his act-first, worry-later attitude?

"You got all that from my dress?" Her brow creased. "You should write those experiences down."

"To what end?" It was one thing to put on a show for his television series; it was another to reflect on his personal experiences. "It was just a motorcycle trip."

"One that few people will have the opportunity to experience. You have a knack for drawing in your audience. It will make your cookbook that much more appealing."

"I'm not doing a cookbook."

"Why not?"

"You know why not."

"Because it would require you to sit still too long. Why don't you collaborate with someone?"

"How about I collaborate with you?"

"Me?"

"Why not? It was your idea."

"I don't know the first thing about creating a cookbook."

"But you could figure out what needed to be done."

"I'm too busy." But after a pause, she added, "We can talk about this after the restaurant opens."

He could see that she was on her way to becoming his partner. Why he'd proposed the idea to her was immediately obvious. She possessed the organization and dedication to detail he lacked. Plus, he trusted her opinion. He could count on one hand how many people fell into that category.

"Fair enough," he said, snagging her fingers with his and drawing her deeper into the kitchen. "Let's get down to why you're here."

"Your menu."

"I thought we'd start with a sea bass." He went on to explain the othcr seven dishes he planned to make for her.

"They all sound wonderful. Good thing I brought my appetite."

He'd prepared his sauces and assembled his ingredients through the afternoon so now it was just a matter of cooking the proteins and assembling the plates. Harper's gaze followed his every move as he shifted between burners and oven. He worked in silence, concentrating on his process, but occasionally felt the pull of her rapt attention.

"Would you mind taking these out to the dining room?" He indicated two of the plates. "I'll follow with the others in a minute."

By the time he had the last of his dishes plated, she'd returned and grabbed three more entrées, leaving the rest for him. He left the kitchen and crossed the dining room to the same table they'd sat at earlier in the day. It was his favorite in the whole restaurant. Quiet, out of the way, but with the vantage of being able to see the whole room.

Candles in crystal holders sent light flickering through the medium-bodied, golden 2006 Chenin Blanc he'd chosen to pair with the sea bass and the truffle risotto. Harper's eyes were bright with wonder as she surveyed their laden table and the assortment of wines he'd opened.

"I'm not sure how we're supposed to eat and drink all this," she said, sounding overwhelmed but delighted.

"It's a buffet. Taste a little of each. Sample the wines. I chose a selection of African vintages for tonight. We'll offer these as well as domestic and foreign."

"I love that your heritage is the backbone of Batouri. When you first told me the name, you explained that the restaurant is named after a town in Africa, but I can't remember where it was located. "

"It's in the East Province of Cameroon."

"Why did you choose it?"

He didn't think she'd like hearing the raw truth, but respected her enough to give her a doctored-up version. "I lived there for three years when I was a teenager."

"It was your home, then."

He poured her a glass of Pinotage. "Try the lamb. It's marinated in yogurt, garlic, coriander seeds, ground cumin and onion."

"Delicious," she murmured, her eyes half closing as she savored the bite.

Ashton couldn't tear his gaze from her face. Her open expression of pure sensual delight shot through him like a laser. Something came undone in his chest. He ached with the unraveling. The temptation to capture her lips with his, to share in her pleasure, swept through him. He reminded himself that a great deal of work had been involved in putting these dishes together. Work that would be for nothing if he acted on his impulse to make love to her right here and now.

He cleared his throat. "I'm glad you like it." His voice had a rough edge as if he'd been cheering on his team in a World Cup final.

"*Love* would be a better word." She sipped the wine and nodded. "This pairs very well with the lamb. What's next?"

Her eagerness made him smile. "Try the duck confit with the Chardonnay."

By the time she'd tasted the final dish, she wore a dreamy, satiated smile. He'd eaten little, preferring to watch her relish every bite. His gut took a hit every time she sighed in appreciation. It was foreplay unlike anything he'd ever known, and he was grateful for the experience.

"Everything was fantastic," she said. "Put it all on the menu. Batouri will be the most sought after reservation in Las Vegas."

He hoped she was right.

"I only have one dessert," he said, watching her take another bite of the scallop crudo with blood orange, watercress and fennel. "I hope you've left room."

"I'll make room."

He left her to fetch the dessert, bringing out only one plate since he doubted she had room for more than a bite or two. "It's a spiced chestnut cake with orange confit."

She accepted the dessert fork he handed her and dug in. "Oh, this is amazing. Are you tired of me telling you how wonderful you are?"

"That could never happen." In fact, he hadn't enjoyed her praise half as much as he'd been happy that his food had moved her to smile and laugh and groan in delight.

She shifted on the seat, turning her torso fully toward him. Taking his face between her hands, she compelled his gaze to hers. The candlelight picked out the amber flecks in her brown eyes, intensifying their compelling power. Slowly, deliberately, she leaned forward until their lips grazed in a dragonfly whisper of a kiss.

"You have an incredible gift. Thank you for sharing it with me tonight."

There was only so much a man could take. Ashton tunneled his fingers into her hair and caught her mouth with a fervent moan of surrender. Greedy for the taste of her, he licked past her lips and was greeted by no resistance, no hesitation, only the delicious slide of her tongue against his.

The layered fruitiness of Chenin Blanc and spiced chestnut danced across his taste buds as Harper tilted her head and gave him deeper access to her mouth. He hadn't realized just how ravenous he was until her arms went around his neck, and she pressed her breasts hard against his chest. Their breath combined in great heaving gasps as one kiss followed another. Drinking his fill of her soft lips seemed impossible. Each second that ticked by he wanted her more.

Dishes rattled on the table as they bumped against it. Distantly, Ashton considered the impracticality of their current location. He'd never be able to get her naked in such a confined space. And that's how he intended she be when he made love to her. Not one inch of her slender frame was

going to go unexplored by him. He'd lain awake too many
nights imagining her flawless skin and how it would feel
to slide his palms against its softness.

He nipped lightly at her throat. Her body jerked reflex-
ively, startling a laugh out of her. When he shifted his grip
from her nape to her spine, his elbow banged the table hard.
A wineglass tipped over.

"Damn it," he muttered.

"It's empty." She leaned back and surveyed the damage
they'd done. "This really isn't the opportune place to get
carried away like that."

"No." Desire shrieked through him, fierce and un-
quenched. He set his spine against the back of the booth
and raked his fingers through his hair. "Damn."

"Let's clean all this up."

"There'll be a cleaning crew coming by at midnight."
He didn't want to leave the intimacy of the candlelit booth
for the harsh fluorescent starkness of the stainless-steel
kitchen.

"Then they'll have less to do." Already she was shifting
out of the booth and piling up the plates.

He paused a second before moving, taking a moment
to survey her high color, mussed hair and the extra bit of
skin bared by their sensual tussling. Damn but she was
glorious. Graceful and romantic, confident and feminine.
If her employees could see her now, would they take her
seriously as a businesswoman? They would if they noticed
the determination in her stare.

"Come on," she said, her tone a stern nudge.

"I suppose the faster we put everything away the sooner
we can get back to the getting acquainted portion of tonight's schedule."

She gave him a *we'll see* smile and headed toward the
kitchen. Ashton quickly bussed the table and followed her,
unconcerned that Harper appeared to be in full retreat. He
had a restaurant to open. That meant he wasn't going any-

where for now. There would be plenty of time to get better acquainted.

Once Harper had deemed the kitchen was organized enough to leave to the cleaners, they shut off the lights and exited the restaurant.

"This has been a nice night," he told her, lacing his fingers through hers. "I don't want it to end."

"If you have in mind a nightcap in your room…" She let the sentence trail off and shook her head.

He couldn't resist a wicked grin. "So, sex is a no." He tugged her close and slipped his fingers into her silky hair, captured her gaze with his and let suspense build. The way her breath hitched, she obviously expected him to push his agenda on her. "How about a walk instead?"

Five

The persistent rattle of her smartphone on the nightstand yanked Harper out of a delicious dream. She had been riding behind Ashton on a motorcycle that was speeding along a coastal highway. Each curve had offered different views of the treacherous terrain ahead, and the exhilarating danger had stolen her breath. Heart still pounding in reaction to the dream, Harper threw her arms wide and stretched, enjoying the slide of cool sheets against her bare skin. Glancing at the clock she saw it was almost nine. She should have been in the office an hour ago. No doubt Mary was frantically looking for her.

With a sigh, Harper slid out of bed and headed straight for the shower. No time to work out this morning. Breaking her routine gave Harper a guilty thrill. So did the reason why she'd turned off the alarm before falling into bed the night before. The walk that Ashton had proposed had lasted two hours. They'd meandered all over the three Fontaine hotels, taking time to tour the gardens at Richesse and have a drink at Chic's chandelier bar.

At first Harper hadn't said much. Mostly she'd asked for the stories that hadn't made it onto the show. Apparently there were hundreds of hours of footage that had gone unseen. Harper would have given a lot to view all of it. She imagined hilarious outtakes and unrehearsed moments of awkwardness. But there would also be bittersweet interviews and breathtaking scenery.

After the walk, they'd ended up at a table in Fontaine Ciel's coffee shop that overlooked the pool area. Ashton had turned the conversation away from him and gleaned a great deal of Harper's history, including her parents' difficult marriage and how she'd coped with finding out about her two half sisters. He'd known she was ambitious, but now he knew the life experiences that had molded her dreams and goals.

It was the most time she'd ever spent with him and by far the least adversarial. Ashton had proven to be an accomplished interviewer and a charming companion. Funny, perceptive and insightful, he'd turned out to be more interesting than she'd expected. And that was saying a lot.

Now a decidedly infatuated woman stared back at Harper when she cleared the steam from the bathroom mirror. Her reflection told her all she needed to know about how much trouble she was in. The last thing she should do was fall for Ashton Croft. Given his track record, he was almost guaranteed to disappoint her in the very near future.

Putting the celebrity chef out of her mind, Harper dressed and picked up her phone. She winced as she read through her emails and texts. A lot of issues needed her attention before noon when she was meeting her sisters. Because Violet hadn't returned home until late yesterday, they'd decided their weekly breakfast should change to lunch this one time.

Harper had taken advantage of this change in her schedule to spend more time with Ashton the night before. One cup of coffee had become two and then three. By the time she tumbled into bed at four in the morning, she'd been far too wired to sleep despite the fact that she'd been drinking decaf the whole time.

But the reduced amount of sleep she'd gotten didn't seem to be affecting her energy level, just her mental capacity. Harper was having a hard time concentrating on all the details competing for her attention.

Lost in daydreams featuring the lush scenery of Indonesia where Ashton had most recently been, she exited her hotel suite and headed to the executive floor. What incredible adventures he'd had. And she hadn't needed to wait another three months to learn about them on his show.

"Harper, are you okay?"

"Hmmm?" She blinked and noticed her assistant was frowning at her. Harper was standing by Mary's desk, but her mind was thousands of miles away. "Sorry. I was thinking about…" Stumped for an excuse, Harper trailed off. She couldn't admit she'd been fantasizing about Ashton Croft and the romantic beaches of Bali. "You were saying?"

"It can wait until this afternoon. Are you planning on coming back here after lunch with your sisters?"

"I think so. Unless something comes up." Rarely was she this indecisive. "I'll call you and let you know."

The walk to Scarlett's office at Fontaine Richesse through the connecting skyways took longer than her usual ten minutes of brisk walking. To maximize the all-inclusive feel of the three hotels, a variety of high-end stores lined the second floor route. The only reason Harper normally paid attention to the boutiques was to eyeball the number of customers and gauge what worked and what didn't. Today, she found herself window-shopping.

A particularly sexy black dress in a front display caught her eye, causing Harper to stop. She didn't need to glance at her watch to know she was running behind schedule, but the need to try on the dress drew her into the store. It wasn't her usual style, but Harper imagined Ashton's eyes

lighting up on Batouri's opening night and knew she had
to have it. She directed the sales clerk to send it to her office at Fontaine Ciel and made arrangements for payment.
She'd need a sexy pair of black stilettos to complete the
look, but those would have to wait until later. She was really late for lunch.

Her sisters wore matching expressions of concern as
Harper entered Scarlett's organized, roomy office.

"Sorry I'm late."

"It's fine," Violet said. "I love your hair down. You
should wear it that way more often."

Harper self-consciously brushed the fine strands away
from her face. "I was in a hurry this morning." That wasn't
exactly true. She'd been reliving the pleasure of Ashton's
fingers playing in her hair. Her skin had tingled as the ends
had swept her shoulder and caressed her cheek.

"So it has nothing to do with your canoodling with Ashton last night?" Scarlett queried, her expression knowing
and smug.

Violet's eyes went wide. "Canoodling?"

"Hardly," Harper said. "We simply went for a walk."

"Sweetie, after my night manager mentioned he'd caught
sight of you with a man last night, I watched video of that
walk," Scarlett teased. "You might not have been touching,
but that was big-time canoodling for you."

The delight fluttering in Harper's stomach was mess-
ing with her head. She tried to shoot her sister a repressive
glare, but felt the corner of her mouth tilted upward. "We
talked until almost four this morning."

"Talked?"

Harper stared Scarlett down. "Talked."

"You mean to tell me Ashton Croft didn't put the moves
on you?"

"He tried." Harper was both relieved and disappointed
that he hadn't put more effort into persuading her to have

that drink in his suite. "I'm not going to hop into bed with him that fast."

Scarlett made a disgusted noise. "That fast? You two have been flirting for nine months."

"Flirting? No. We've been politely fighting."

"For you that's flirting."

Harper threw up her hand to block any more of her sister's crazy notions. "Is there a particular reason there's a bottle of champagne chilling over there?"

"We have a lot to celebrate, starting with Violet," Scarlett explained. She poured the sparkling liquid into three flutes and motioned her sisters over.

"You were able to help JT get his company back, weren't you," Harper guessed, delighted.

The smirk on Violet's face was priceless. "And Preston has been arrested. He was dragged out of Cobalt in handcuffs."

"I would have loved to see the look on his face as he was escorted out of his hotel by the FBI," said Harper.

Violet nodded. "It was pretty satisfying."

"And things between you and JT?" Scarlett prompted.

"Perfect."

Harper's heart lifted at the joy on her sister's face. "You're not separating then."

"Not a chance." Fierce and romantic, Violet beamed. "He loves me."

"I'm happy for you," Harper said, but already she was worrying about how this would change things between the three of them. "Have you figured out what's going to happen when JT takes over Stone Properties?"

"He's not. Once his father was out of the way I thought for sure that JT would step in as CEO." The sole reason Violet had married JT was to help him take over his family's company. "Instead, he sold his shares to his cousin in order to buy Titanium." Titanium was the Stone Properties hotel and casino JT ran in Las Vegas. It was the largest and most profitable of all the company's properties, thanks to JT's excellent management.

Harper couldn't see the sense in his decision. "I'm surprised he would do that when he could have all of Stone Properties to run."

"He wanted to stay in Las Vegas." Violet looked as blissful as a woman in love should. "He knew my heart was here."

"What about Grandfather's contest?" Harper asked. The corporate offices for Fontaine Hotels and Resorts were in New York City.

"Last week I told Grandfather I wasn't interested in being CEO." Violet looked at Scarlett.

Before Harper grasped what Violet's decision meant for the future, Scarlett held her glass high and proclaimed, "All hail the future CEO of Fontaine Hotels and Resorts."

Harper's heart twisted in her chest. Had Grandfather made his decision? Was Scarlett his choice for a successor?

"Congratulations," Harper said to Scarlett, proud that her voice was so bright when her heart was lost in shadow. She'd wanted Grandfather to pick her, had spent her entire life working toward that goal. More than that, she needed his acceptance. To think that she wasn't good enough was a blow she hadn't prepared herself for.

Scarlett rolled her eyes. "Not me, silly. You."

"Me?" Harper looked from Scarlett to Violet. "I don't understand. Grandfather hasn't said anything about the contest being over."

Scarlett piped up. "I called Grandfather this morning and told him that the network executives loved the pilot for my new series and picked up the show." Her starlet smile flashed bold and brilliant. "That means you are going to be Fontaine's next CEO."

The news should have thrilled Harper. It was why she'd worked hard and sacrificed a social life in high school to ensure she got into Cornell University's School of Hotel

Administration. After graduating with top honors she'd gone to work at a Fontaine property in Chicago, starting at the bottom to learn every aspect of the business. All her energy had gone into proving to her grandfather that she was not her father's daughter. She would give Fontaine Hotels and Resorts her complete attention.

But to get the job because her competition had dropped out. That wasn't her idea of winning.

"Grandfather still has the final word," she reminded her sisters, not ready to celebrate. "He might just decide that I wasn't going to be his first choice."

"Don't be ridiculous," Scarlett scoffed, clinking her crystal flute with Harper's. "You are and always have been the front-runner." She glanced at Violet. "No offense, Violet. I think if you'd hung in there you might have given Harper a run for her money."

"I'm not insulted," Violet said, a fond look in her eyes. "I love Las Vegas. And I love running my hotel. I'm not really cut out to sit in endless meetings and read reports all day." But Harper knew Violet was downplaying how serious her decision had been.

At Scarlett's urging, Harper sipped at the sparkling wine, but the effervescent liquid didn't ignite joy or even relief. As soon as Ashton's restaurant opened, she would head to New York and have a face-to-face chat with her grandfather. Until she knew his thoughts on her future with the company, she wouldn't let herself hope her dreams were coming true.

In a state of conflicting emotions, Harper ate her salad in silence and listened to Violet and Scarlett with half her attention. Both of them were madly in love with wonderful men. It was hard for Harper to contribute to the conversation. Listening to them discuss Violet's upcoming belated honeymoon and Scarlett's wedding arrangements demonstrated just how two-dimensional Harper's life was. She had her work and her sisters. Both meant everything to her, but after spending the evening with Ashton, she couldn't help feeling as if she was missing out on something important.

"I got an update from Logan a little before you showed up today," Scarlett said, catching Harper's eye. "He said his people have tracked the million your mother wired to the blackmailer." Scarlett didn't explain how this had been done and Harper refrained from asking, expecting that the methods were not official. "It went through several banks before it landed in an account belonging to some guy named Saul Eddings. The strange part is he doesn't seem to exist."

So, the blackmailer was clever. Harper had been racking her brains for days trying to figure out who could have dug up a thirty-year-old affair. Why wait until now to trade the information for money?

"What's going on?" Violet asked.

"My mother is being blackmailed."

"Your mother?" Violet shot Scarlett a worried look. "Blackmailed about what?"

"Ancient history," Harper explained, wondering what was causing Violet's escalating tension. "Apparently she had an affair thirty years ago."

Violet whirled on Scarlett. "You didn't tell her, did you?"

"No." Scarlett eyes grew hard as she stared at Violet.

"She needs to know."

"I need to know what?" Harper demanded, alarmed by the sudden animosity between her sisters.

"It won't help," Scarlett said. "Logan will find out who's doing this and he and Lucas will take care of it. So, you need to just let it go."

"Have you thought of what's best for Harper?"

"Repeatedly." Scarlett could be a force of nature when she sank her teeth into something. "Drop it."

Harper couldn't take it anymore. "Stop it, both of you.

I need to know what's going on. Who's blackmailing my mother?"

"I don't know," Scarlett admitted, as somber as Harper had ever seen her.

Harper persisted. "But you know something about it."

"I think so."

"And you weren't planning on telling me?" The room suddenly felt cold, as if the air conditioners were working at twice their normal capacity. Harper rubbed her arms. "Why?"

"Because no good will come of it," Scarlett said.

All the more reason for her to know. "It's about my mother and the affair?"

"Yes." Violet reached out and took Harper's icy fingers, rubbing them to bring back some warmth. "Tiberius had files on all of us."

"I already knew that."

"Including your mother."

"When I was attacked and the files were stolen," Scarlett explained, her voice quiet and reluctant, "the one on your mother was taken."

"That explains where the photos came from and why the blackmail began now." One question answered. But was that all there was to the sharp looks and tense exchange between Violet and Scarlett? "Is there more to it?"

"If you don't tell her, I will," Violet declared.

"It's about the timing of the affair," Scarlett said. "It happened nine months before you were born."

"That doesn't mean…" Harper wasn't sure she wanted to make the connections Scarlett was hinting at. "The affair only lasted two weeks."

"And from what we've determined about your father's travels, he was gone for almost six weeks around that same time."

Bile rose in Harper's throat. It couldn't be possible. It certainly wasn't fair.

She wasn't a Fontaine.

These two wonderful women weren't her sisters.

She had no right to run Fontaine Ciel, much less become CEO of the company.

Suddenly, Harper couldn't breathe. She put her hand to her chest. "I have to go."

She pushed back from the table so abruptly her chair crashed to the ground. Scarlett's office spun as Harper struggled to figure out where the door had gone.

"Harper, are you okay?"

Okay? Would she ever be okay again?

"Fine. I just remembered that I was going to…" She never finished the sentence. The door had come into view and Harper made for it.

"Are you sure you're all right?" Violet had pursued her from Scarlett's office into the hallway. "I know this must be a huge shock. But it doesn't matter. You know that."

"Of course it matters." Harper didn't know how to make Violet understand. Everything she'd worked for. Every sacrifice she'd made. Was it all for nothing? "I'll talk to you and Scarlett later. Right now I just need to grab some air."

Scarlett appeared on Harper's other side, her fingers biting hard into Harper's arm. "You are our sister. You will be Fontaine's next CEO. It's what you've always wanted."

"Of course." Harper patted Scarlett's hand. "I get it. This is our secret."

Violet relaxed. "Exactly."

"I love you both, but I need to get back to work. I'll check in with you later."

And before they could protest further, she briskly walked away.

Instead of retracing her steps through the skyways, she wound through the casino and emerged onto the Vegas Strip. The heat, noise and press of the crowd hit her like a rogue wave. How long had it been since she'd ventured beyond the insulation of Fontaine walls? She slept, ate and worked within a square city block, finding little need to explore the world outside. There was a drugstore attached to the hotel if she needed sundries. When she traveled, it was in a hired car that swept her to the airport and a private plane that carried her to her destination.

Always there was someone around to guide her to meetings and keep her on schedule. She'd never detoured because the mood hadn't struck her. Her activities were planned and organized. It was the way she liked it. What had made her successful.

With more vigor than necessary, Harper pushed through the ground floor door that led into Fontaine Ciel's casino. Nothing looked familiar. The persistent noise from the slot machines and the dazzling lights battered her senses. She had no idea how to get to her office. Disoriented, Harper turned in a slow circle. Confusion overwhelmed her. Harper put her arms out for balance as the edges of her vision began to darken.

"Harper, are you okay?"

She couldn't remember the name of the man who spoke. Distantly she knew she should. That she dealt with him on a daily basis. Tom something. Tim maybe.

"I'm a little dizzy all of a sudden." She shook her head, hoping to clear her vision. To her right was an open slot machine. "I just need to sit down for a second." She took a step and swayed.

"Let me help," Tom or Tim said, reaching for her arm.

She flinched away from his touch. Her skin felt as if it was on fire. "No." She reached the chair and dropped into it. "Sorry. I'll be fine in a couple seconds. Perhaps you could get me a glass of water."

"Sure."

While he headed off to intercept a waitress, Harper closed her eyes and rubbed at her temples. Her brain was coming back online, allowing her to think more clearly. What the hell had just happened? From her symptoms she guessed it had been a panic attack. Made sense. Her whole world was spinning out of control.

By the time Tim Hoffman—she'd finally recalled the name of her facilities manager—returned with her water, Harper was on her feet and feeling much steadier. But her need to run hadn't abated. For someone who always met problems head-on, she wasn't sure what to make of the impulse to flee. Work wasn't the remedy for her troubles. It was the cause of her angst. Better that she spend some time alone. To think. To sort out her emotions.

"I should have taken the skyway back from Richesse. Must have been the heat outside that made me dizzy."

The short, dark-haired man looked relieved. "It's warmer than usual, that's for sure."

"Thanks for the water." Without another word, Harper headed for the elevators. Maybe an hour on her treadmill would enable her to reach some clarity.

Six

Ashton stretched out on the couch in his suite and stared at the ceiling. Beyond the wall of windows the day was fading and the Las Vegas Strip was lighting up. As much as he loved the fascinating sights he'd seen in some of the most remote spots on the planet, enjoying the luxury of a first-class hotel was an indulgence he appreciated most of all.

Unfortunately, his current career issues weren't allowing him to put aside his worries and savor the lavender scented sheets, decadent bathroom or spectacular view. Vince had called this morning with bad news. Unless the producers of *The Culinary Wanderer* received his decision about filming in Africa three days from now they were cancelling the show.

As much as Ashton hated having anyone force his hand, he should be relieved that he would soon be free to sign with the Lifestyle Network. He and Phillips could part without bad feelings. But if everything was so great, why did he feel numb?

A knock sounded on his door. Shoving to a sitting position, Ashton ran his fingers through his hair and got to his feet. Dae had said he'd call later and see if Ashton wanted to check out the Strip. He hadn't expected the kid to show up.

But it wasn't Dae. The visitor at his door was so unexpected, he stood staring at her in dumfounded silence.

"Hi." Harper stood in the hallway wearing stretchy gray pants that highlighted her long, lean legs and an oversized pale pink sweater that she wrapped tight around her body. "I probably should have called before stopping by." Her casual attire and indecisive posture meant she hadn't come here to talk business.

"No need. I was just thinking that I could use a little company." He gestured her inside.

"That's how I felt, too." She shuffled in and gazed around the suite as if she hadn't been instrumental in overseeing every aspect of the design and decor. Sounding dreamy and vague, she continued. "I enjoyed our conversation last night."

"So did I." Catching her hand, he drew her toward the couch. "Do you want some wine?"

"Sure."

He poured glasses for both of them and sat close beside her. Content to enjoy her company, Ashton sipped his wine and watched her. She wore no makeup and that added to the aura of vulnerability that surrounded her at the moment. The scent of jasmine clung to her skin. A trace of damp lingered in the thick wave of brown hair cascading around her delicate shoulders. He guessed she'd been working out recently for a healthy glow suffused her skin.

"Did you always want to be a chef?" With her feet tucked beneath her, she took up very little space, but vibrancy had returned to her voice.

"I sort of stumbled into it."

The truth wanted to spill out of him. Last night she'd shared a great deal about her childhood and school years.

Her openness had tempted him to talk about his own past. But most of the people who knew what he'd done had either been dumped in the African jungle or buried in a shallow grave. An elegant, cultured woman like Harper would be horrified by what it had cost him to survive.

"When I was fifteen," he began, abandoning the press release version of his past, "I left home and fell in with some bad guys."

Describing Chapman's ruthless gang of smugglers as bad guys was woefully inadequate. They'd been a mean bunch of criminals brought together by the most loathsome man Ashton had ever met.

"How bad?"

He pushed back his left sleeve and showed her a pair of long, faint scars on his forearm. "They liked to play with knives."

"They did this to you? That doesn't look much like playing. Why did you stick around?"

"Because I was cocky and stubborn. I thought I could take care of myself." And he'd had nowhere else to go. Ashton brushed his sleeve down. "One of the guys did all the cooking for the gang. He took me under his wing. Kept me away from the worst of the lot. Turns out I had a knack for combining flavors." Not the whole truth, just a sterilized version of what had really happened.

"Had you planned to do anything else?"

Ashton shrugged. He'd been a stupid, rebellious teenager who'd rarely thought beyond the moment. "I only knew I wasn't going to follow in my father's footsteps."

Her lips twisted into an unhappy grimace. "What did he do?"

"He was a missionary." He hadn't planned to disclose that fact. Usually, he told people his father was a salesman. Which was pretty close to the truth. His parents spent their whole lives selling salvation to people who had no idea they were damned.

For the first time since she'd arrived on his doorstep, her eyes brightened. "A missionary? Forgive me if I say that you don't strike me as the son of a religious man."

She made no attempt to hide her curiosity. Nor did she curb the trace of laughter in her tone. This wasn't the withdrawn, mentally drained woman who'd shown up at his door. The cloud that had followed her into his suite had retreated for the moment.

"I could say I'm not and explain that there are all sorts of missionaries in Africa, but my father and mother spent a great deal of my childhood visiting villages and spreading Christian values."

His muscles grew more taut with each syllable that passed his lips. He began to notice an ache in his shoulders. The pain reminded him that he'd never set down the burden of unfinished business created by his choice to leave home and never look back.

"Wow, that was not a happy memory for you at all." She set her fingertips on his forearm, her touch light and friendly.

Too bad his heart didn't recognize the contact as casual. It gave a giant lurch like a racehorse surging from a starting gate. In seconds his breath came more quickly. Usually when desire hit him, he rolled with the blow. Why resist? Beautiful women were their own type of adventure.

But Harper Fontaine wasn't just a beautiful woman. She was intelligent and ambitious, dynamic and resourceful. When he'd first started working with her, he'd been annoyed by her bluntness and impressed by her sincerity. Last night he'd discovered she was also a warm, passionate woman and the chemistry between them was electrifying.

"What about you?" he asked, turning the topic away from himself. "Did you always want to be a hotel executive?"

"From the time I was five years old." She smiled fondly. "My father took me to the Waldorf Astoria and I fell in love. It was everything a grand hotel should be. We went at Christmas and the lobby was filled with these enormous evergreen trees covered in white lights and big red and gold balls. The railings were decorated with swags of ribbon and lights. It was magical. I knew I wanted to be a part of that someday."

He had little trouble imagining her as a wide-eyed child, holding tight to her father's hand while she soaked up the magnificence of that fine old hotel. For her, it had probably been as exciting a place to visit as FAO Schwarz would be for most other children.

"I suppose being a Fontaine, hotels are in your blood."

Her expression changed—the glow in her eyes dimmed, her mouth flattening into a somber line. "What's it like traveling all over the world like you do?"

"Exciting. Exhausting." Sometimes he longed to go home. Or at least that's what he assumed he wanted. He never really felt as if he belonged anywhere. "I crave an ever-changing landscape."

"That's so different from what I'm used to." Setting her elbow on the back of the couch, she propped her head on her hand and sipped her wine. "I've never traveled anywhere."

"I find that hard to believe. There are Fontaine hotels all over the world."

"Yes, but when I've visited the hotels I've never had time to sightsee. You said you couldn't see me shopping in Paris. You were right. I've been there three times and never once toured the city."

"That's a shame. It's a wonderful city. I spent two years there attending culinary school and working in various restaurants." It had been the first place he'd gone after leaving South Africa. At the time, it had seemed the perfect place to re-create himself.

"I spent the first eighteen years of my life in New York City and the next four in Ithaca attending Cornell University."

"You didn't want to travel?"

"My parents were separated from the time I was eleven. My mother lived in Florida, and I visited her during the holidays. My father..." She stumbled over the word and appeared distressed for a moment. "He was gone a lot, overseeing various hotels. The company expanded a great deal in the nineties."

Her childhood sounded as lonely as his had been. "Who did you stay with when your father was away?"

"Servants. Once in a while my grandfather." Her sweater had slipped off one shoulder, baring the thin strap of her gray camisole. "Is there any place you want to visit but haven't?"

The smooth line of her shoulder captivated him. Could her skin be as soft as it looked? "Niagara Falls."

She stared at him in stunned silence for a few moments and then began to laugh. "Niagara Falls? Even I've been there."

Her deep, throaty laugh made him want to kiss her. The mischief dancing in her eyes captivated him. Strong. Soft. Smart. Sexy. Was she as oblivious to her appeal as she appeared or was it all a ruse to catch him off guard?

"Then you'd be a good tour guide."

"I don't know about that. I was seven at the time." Her good mood faded. "My father took me." She blinked rapidly and pushed off the couch. "Damn it. I swore I wasn't going to cry."

Curiosity induced him to follow her. At least that's what he told himself until she was wrapped in his arms, her face pressed against his chest. Her body shuddered as she gulped in air and released an unsteady sigh.

"What's wrong?" He nuzzled the top of her head with his chin while a part of his mind wondered where this urge to comfort had come from. Selfish. Self-involved. Those were the words that described him. It balanced out the fifteen years of selflessness his parents had shoved down his throat.

"Why Niagara Falls?"

"I have a thing for waterfalls." He paused a beat. "What do you have a thing for?"

"You…" she shifted as far away from him as his arms snaked around her waist would allow "…r show."

"Nice save."

"Okay, I'll admit I'm a fan."

He leaned back and peered down at her. "That explains why you've been so nice to me."

"I've been nothing but professional to you."

"Your lips say civilized things," he taunted. "But your eyes tell me how much you'd like to lock me in the walk-in freezer."

"Be honest. Have you been easy to work with?"

"Of course not, but I'm a genius and everyone knows that geniuses are notoriously difficult to get along with."

His candor gave her pause. Head cocked, she regarded him. "Even your arrogance is charming."

"I don't get you."

She avoided his gaze. "What's there to get?"

"You have money and family connections. Anything you want could be yours."

"Is that how you see me?" She asked the question calmly enough, but below the surface he sensed tension.

"That's who you are."

"And if I lacked money and family connections, what am I then?"

The intensity with which she awaited his answer kept Ashton from spouting some flippant remark. "A beautiful, intelligent woman who is ambitious and focused enough to do anything she sets her mind to."

"What if I don't know what I want to do?"

"I don't understand. I thought you were going to take over as CEO of Fontaine Hotels and Resorts."

"I'm no longer sure that's where I belong." She pushed out of his arms and headed toward the door to the hallway. "Thanks for the wine and the shoulder to cry on. I should turn in for the night. I've got a lot to do tomorrow."

Ashton followed her to the door and caught her arm as she reached for the handle, stopping her from leaving. She turned at his touch and swayed into him. Pushing onto her toes, she kissed his cheek.

The warmth of her lips against his skin set his blood alight. His fingers slid into the small of her back and held her against him as he cupped her cheek in his palm and angled her face so he could reach her mouth.

Pliant and slightly salty from her earlier tears, her lips moved beneath his, responding to his searching kiss. It wasn't passion that consumed him. Her somber mood connected him to an emotion he believed he'd lost long ago: compassion. Something radical had happened to her today. Something related to the visit from her mother. The encounter had knocked her off her game.

Just like this kiss was throwing him.

He lifted his lips from hers, shocked by his lightheadedness. One simple kiss shouldn't have affected him so strongly. But then again, he couldn't remember wanting to kiss away someone's unhappiness, either.

"Stay," he urged, brushing his lips across her cheek.

Her muscles tensed. A flight response?

"That's not a good idea."

"You're wrong," he assured her. "It's a great idea."

"I've never jumped into bed with a man I scarcely know."

He'd divulged the truth about his parents with her. That was a huge secret from his past he hadn't shared with anyone else in his present. "Consider it an adventure into the unfamiliar territory."

"I guess I'm not ready to leave behind everything I know."

Yet another enigmatic statement. Ashton was starting to think that Harper had more weighing on her mind than she wanted to confront.

"Why would you think you have to?"

"I don't need to ask you what you'd do if you couldn't be a chef. You've already made a name for yourself as a TV personality and a restaurateur."

This would have been an excellent moment to tell her his project was taking him to New York for a few days, but he was reluctant to shatter the rapport between them.

"Have you been considering a career change?"

A faint smile found its way to her lips. "I was thinking of a television series that featured exotic hotels around the world."

"Want me to talk to my manager about pitching your idea to the network?"

Her eyes widened. "You're serious."

"You seem as if you're grappling with the status quo. Maybe you need to take some risks, challenge yourself. Do something that terrifies you."

"I've already done that." Her expression grew wry. "I came here, didn't I?"

"I terrify you?"

"Not you. Just what you represent."

"And that is?"

"Everything that I grew up avoiding."

He didn't respond to her jab. Better to give her space to assemble her thoughts, let the silence expand to an uncomfortable level until she gave up more than she intended. It was an interview technique he'd often used with great results.

"I didn't mean that as an insult," she said at last. "It's just that I like everything organized and predictable. You thrive on the unexpected."

"It's what makes life interesting. Some of my best recipes have come from putting together flavors that I've never tried before." Hell, his entire career had been framed by a combination of happenstance and his ability to capitalize on all things unconventional. "And I never would've made a career out of cooking if I hadn't run away from home at fifteen and needed to survive."

She didn't look at all surprised by what he'd told her. "I've never wanted to be in a desperate situation, so I never have been." The rest of her admission remained unspoken, but her expression was easy to read.

"And now you're wondering what you've missed?"

"I'm fully aware of what I've missed. I've made sacrifices to keep on track with my goal."

"To run the company someday."

"It was my job to win or lose."

"Has that changed?"

"You must have guessed that it has or I wouldn't have come here tonight and cried all over you." She stepped back and gathered her soft sweater tight about her slim body. "I found out something today that I'm not ready to talk about."

"Use me as a sounding board or keep everything bottled up. It's no matter to me."

"I guess I should say thank you."

"There's no need. As you probably already figured out, I'm a selfish bastard. If a beautiful woman comes to me for comfort, I'm going to enjoy every second of the time she spends in my arms."

"And if she decides to let you comfort her through the night?"

"All the better."

"How do women manage to resist you?"

"Usually they don't."

"So I'm an anomaly?"

"In a class all of your own."

She put her hand on the door handle once again, and this time Ashton didn't stop her. He'd learned to coax the flavor out of food. Forcing something to happen often led to an inferior outcome and above all else, he wanted the first time he made love to Harper to be a moment she'd never forget.

Harper couldn't make herself open the door. Her body ached for his touch. Last night when they'd kissed she'd been able to resist him—just barely. But she'd been nervous about being discovered and had no intention of being seen accompanying Ashton to his suite.

Would it be any better if she was seen exiting his suite in the morning? No, but she was on the verge of not caring.

He must have picked up on her ambivalence because he gently pried her fingers from the handle and dropped a sizzling kiss in her palm. She melted beneath the heat of his gaze and didn't protest when his fingers sought the small of her back. Nor did she resist when with a soft groan he pulled her torso up and firmly into his body.

"Ask me again to stay," she whispered, exhilarated by the leashed passion vibrating in Ashton's muscles.

She dug her fingers into his biceps as he set his open mouth on her neck. The sweep of his tongue against her skin made her moan. Her breasts felt heavy as his arm tightened around her, his chest pushing into her as his breath deepened. The burn beneath her skin made the touch of her clothes unbearable. She needed them gone. Needed to feel his naked flesh against her.

She was half out of her mind with hunger by the time he murmured, "Stay."

"Okay."

He swept her off her feet before the word faded. The air around her cooled as his long, rapid strides brought them to the bedroom. With gentleness she never imagined he possessed, he laid her on the mattress and braced his hands on either side of her head. Wondering what he was up to, she peered at his looming form from beneath her lashes. The intensity of his stare ramped up her desire to be utterly devoured by him.

Raising one hand, she traced the faint hollow of his dimple with her fingertips. The corner of his mouth lifted in response to her touch, deepening the sexy indent. He leaned over her to rub his lips over hers in a tantalizing caress. With an encouraging murmur, she slid her fingers into his hair and brought him closer, deepening the kiss.

Tongues dancing, mouths fused as the heat between them increased, Harper decided the reality of Ashton Croft's kisses was so much better than any fantasy. She wanted to savor the feel of his lips on hers forever, but already her body needed more. Working blindly, she slipped all his shirt buttons free and stroked the fabric off his shoulders. A purr of satisfaction rumbled from her as her palms coasted over the hills and valleys of muscle from his collarbone to his belt.

He seized her lip between his teeth and bit lightly before licking the tender spot. Standing up, he stripped off his shirt, shed his pants and shoes. She scrambled to her knees and peeled off her sweater, but in her haste got her arms caught. Turning the soft knit inside out, she freed herself in time to meet the rush of Ashton's lips as he rejoined her on the bed.

In a jumble of limbs, they rolled across the mattress. Somehow Harper ended up on top. Breathless and laughing, she pressed her lips against Ashton's throat. His hands coasted over her butt and down the backs of her thighs, urging her against the erection straining his boxer briefs. Her head spun as she waited to see where his fingers would explore next.

When they dipped below the waistband of her yoga pants and followed the seam between her butt cheeks to the molten core of her, she gasped. As fleeting as his touch was, it seared her through. She whimpered a protest as he retreated, palms gliding back over the same path. This time he caressed upward, riding the hem of her camisole up over her rib cage.

Almost too shaken to move, but dying to feel his hands on her breasts, Harper placed her palms on the mattress and shoved herself upward. As she'd hoped, he claimed her breasts in his large hands, sending wave after wave of acute pleasure surging through her with his firm touch. She ducked her head as he finished removing her top and emerged from the folds of fabric with a jubilant cry. The sound was cut short as Ashton rolled her beneath him and pulled her nipple into his mouth.

First he sucked, and then swirled his tongue around her nipple, the sensation heightening the lust rampaging through her. She combed her fingers into his hair and held him close. From her throat, mindless, encouraging sounds erupted. She was beyond words. Completely at his command. Whatever he wanted from her she'd give him.

Why had she denied herself this amazing experience for so long? She should have slept with him the first day they met and every time after that. Obviously she wasn't thinking straight because she'd completely forgiven him for all those months of frustration.

Ashton shifted his attention to her second breast and devoted a considerable amount of time driving her desire to alarming heights. His fingers were as busy as his mouth, tracing the skin across her belly, making her stomach muscles pitch and roll. At last he hooked her waistband and applied pressure downward. Harper lifted her hips off the bed to make his job easier. He peeled her pants down her legs, and she finished removing them with three frantic kicks.

His tongue dipped into her navel. Sensation lanced downward. He shifted his broad shoulders between her thighs and used his thumbs to part her folds. Harper clutched the sheets just as his mouth settled over her. Her body jolted, the movement wringing a murmur from her. That's all she had strength for. The rest of her energy was focused on the amazing thing he was doing with his tongue.

Sex wasn't usually on her weekly agenda. She found it

difficult to make time to indulge in a decadent spa treatment or take an afternoon and go shopping. Finding a man she was attracted to seemed far too challenging a prospect, so she went long periods of time without being intimate with anyone.

When first Scarlett and then Violet had fallen in love, Harper might never admit it out loud, but she had envied their glow, the satisfied glint in their eye. Nor had it helped that she'd just begun working with the roguishly handsome Ashton Croft. Hormones long asleep had begun to stir with ever-increasing agitation.

She'd put his ability to exasperate her down to their differing approaches, but with Ashton's mouth sending her into orbit she realized it had just been sexual chemistry and she'd been too long absorbed in her work to recognize the signs.

As pleasure rose, she planted her feet against the mattress and hung on for dear life. His fingers flexed into the soft flesh of her butt, his firm grasp the perfect catalyst to send her spinning out of control. She cried his name as her body exploded. For a second there was a burst of light behind her eyes, and then it slowly faded and she drifted in darkness.

Dimly she felt Ashton shift away from her, but she couldn't move, couldn't protest his leaving. Dimly, she heard the rustle of a condom wrapper and was glad that he'd thought to protect them both. Very few seconds passed before the mattress dipped again. Her lashes fluttered upward as he moved over her once more. His mouth stroked across her lips, tongue dipping between them to tease and arouse all over. Harper put her arms around his shoulders as he shifted his hips between her thighs.

She felt him nudge against her entrance and raised up to meet his thrust as he pushed inside her in one fluid movement. Her inner muscles shuddered in delight, and Ashton buried his face in her neck with a ragged sigh. He was not a small man, and she was a little shocked that her body was able to take him fully. But the rightness of their joining was not to be denied.

Slowly, he started to move. Finding his rhythm took her barely any time at all. Soon it was as if they'd made love a hundred times. She ran her hands over him, finding spots that excited him. He adjusted the angle of her hips and drove into her a little more forcefully. The evocative twist he gave as he plunged into her over and over quickly brought Harper back to the brink of release. As it swept up to claim her once again, she clutched Ashton's forearms and welcomed the frenzied pounding of his body into her as he, too, closed in on his orgasm.

They didn't quite climax together, but it was awfully close. Harper felt the first spasm hit her and dug her nails into Ashton's skin. He kissed her long and hard and with two deep thrusts emptied himself into her with a powerful shudder.

Stunned by the power of what had just happened between them, Harper buried her nose in Ashton's neck and held on while his body trembled. Her sparse personal life hadn't given her a lot of experience in these sorts of matters, but Harper was pretty sure Ashton was as moved as she was.

So what came next?

As if in answer to her question, Ashton shifted his lax muscles and collapsed onto the mattress beside her. They lay side by side, staring up at the ceiling. Harper listened as his breath returned to normal. Her skin was cooling fast. She needed to decide whether to put on her clothes and get out of here or to snuggle against Ashton. Before she'd made up her mind, his fingers closed over hers.

"Don't run off just yet."

Harper turned her head and realized he was watching her. "You don't know that's what I was thinking."

"Don't I?" He rolled onto his side and caught her around

the waist, pulling her beneath him. "Tell me you weren't going to make the excuse that you had to get back to work."

With his warm skin pressing against hers, she knew her opportunity to make a clean getaway had just vanished. Surrendering to the pleasure of his large body overwhelming her, she slid her hands along his muscular arms and marveled at the beauty of his broad shoulders. Already her body craved to be possessed by his once more. He was going to be a hard man to get over.

"I wasn't."

"That doesn't sound much like the Harper I know." He drew back so he could look into her face. "What's happened?"

"I'm pretty sure I'm not the Harper anyone knows."

"I don't understand."

"I found out something today." She pressed her lips together, knowing she shouldn't talk about her secret. If the truth about her paternity got out, she'd never become the CEO of Fontaine Hotels and Resorts. "Something that has changed everything I thought I ever knew about myself."

"That sounds troubling." He stroked her cheek with the tips of his fingers. "What are you going to do?"

Most people would have asked what she'd discovered. With what she'd learned about him in these past few days, Harper understood why he didn't pry. He had a past he wanted to keep private. Things he wasn't proud of.

"I don't know," she told him. "I haven't been thinking too clearly these past few hours." She gave him a wry grin. "I mean, look at me. Twenty-four hours earlier, would I have slept with you?"

"I like to think you were heading down that road."

And she probably had been. "Maybe I'm just making excuses for doing something I've wanted all along."

"Why do you have to make excuses?"

"I don't take sex lightly. For me it's something that comes out of a relationship that has the chance of lasting."

"And you don't think ours will?"

"I think our business relationship will be a lasting one."

He kissed her lightly on the mouth. "I hope so. As for the other, I think we are good for each other. Let's hold on to that for the time being."

As promises went, it wasn't much, but Harper reasoned that for Ashton it was major. She snuggled against his body and let the rhythmic thump of his heart mesmerize her into complete relaxation. The shock of earlier revelations faded as did her ambivalence about what the future held. In Ashton's arms she knew exactly who she was. More than that could wait until the next day.

Seven

Ashton was on his second cup of coffee when the sound of a knock at the door of his suite made him smile. So, after sneaking off while he slept at some point during the wee hours, she'd decided to come back for round four. Smirking, Ashton went to let her in. Only, it wasn't Harper standing in the hall, but Vince.

"What's going on?" he asked his manager, not liking the grim expression Vince wore. "How come you're here?"

"The Lifestyle people have moved up the taping date on your pilot. They want you to come to New York and do it tomorrow."

Ashton cursed, disliking that they were making him jump through hoops. "What's going on?"

"I don't know. We might have dug our heels in a little too hard. I heard they may be looking at other chefs."

And he was going to lose this fantastic opportunity if he didn't move quickly. "What can we do?"

"I'd suggest that we show them how committed we are to Lifestyle Network."

"You want me to quit *The Culinary Wanderer*."

"You're not happy with the direction they intend to take the show next year. I think it's a good time to cut ties."

His gut told him this was the wrong thing to do, but he'd hired Vince because his gut wasn't right 100 percent of the time. Nor was Ashton convinced he could make decisions about the show he'd worked on for so many years without letting his emotions get the better of him.

"Call Phillips and tell them I'm not going to continue with *The Culinary Wanderer*." Harper's face flashed before his eyes as he said this. She would be disappointed. And that bothered him more than it should. But this was business. In the end she'd accept that.

"I have things to do before I can head to New York." Chef Cole had not yet arrived from Chicago to take up his duties. Ashton would brief Dae on all the things that needed to be done in the next few days. The kid was smart and resourceful. "How did you get here?"

"Commercial. The network is sending their plane to pick us up tonight."

Well, at least that was one thing he didn't have to worry about. The biggest challenge was going to be telling Harper that he was leaving ten days before Batouri was due to open. That was a conversation he'd better have sooner than later.

After leaving Ashton slumbering peacefully in his bed, Harper had spent the rest of the night on her couch, burrowed beneath a cotton throw, watching one episode after another of *The Culinary Wanderer*. She'd stared at Ashton's image on the screen, unable to believe she'd fulfilled the only sexual fantasy she'd ever had.

Reality had far exceeded anything she could have dreamed up. She'd expected Ashton would be a skilled and masterful lover, but he'd demonstrated a level of caring and consideration of her pleasure that had far surpassed any intimacy she'd ever known. Even now, after several rounds of lovemaking, her body throbbed with desire for him.

But would she have made love with him last night if her defenses hadn't been crushed by the knowledge that she wasn't a Fontaine? The answer wasn't clear enough for Harper's liking. She felt lost and adrift. It's why she couldn't sleep, couldn't make her mind function the way it normally did. No patterns emerged out of the chaos of her thoughts. Her ability to plan and make things happen had left her. She was a shell, waiting to be filled with purpose.

Harper passed her hand over her dry, tired eyes before levering herself off the cushions and heading to make coffee. Her cell phone chirped. A text message. Probably Mary wondering why she hadn't picked up the report on last night's numbers.

Harper picked up the phone, intending to shut it off. For the first time in her life, she didn't feel like being responsible. But she really should call Mary. Unless Harper explicitly stated her unavailability, her assistant expected her to answer, and if she didn't, Mary would probably send security to check on her.

Heaving a sigh, Harper dialed. With Fontaine Ciel open and running smoothly, she could hand over the reins to her general manager for a while. When her assistant picked up, Harper said, "I'm going to take some time off. If anything comes up have Bob handle it."

As simple as that, she was free. She'd expected to feel lighter with the concerns of the hotel off her shoulders, but it was only a matter of time before her hours of playing hooky would end and she'd take up the reins once more.

Mug in hand, she headed off to shower. In the past ten hours she'd watched the entire season Ashton had spent in Europe. She'd chosen these particular episodes to watch because she'd visited several of the same countries. The contrast between her experiences and his could not have been more dramatic. He loved what he did. The people he met fascinated him. His culinary encounters often astonished him. Not everything was to his taste, but he was always game to try.

She'd visited and left countries without ever getting to know their cultures. Most of the time she was on a tight deadline that left little room to go exploring. She'd been proud of how hard she worked, had wallowed in her arrogance that she knew best in almost every situation.

In her own way, she was as committed to her path as Ashton was to his. She'd grown impatient with his lack of focus on the restaurant. How many people had she frustrated with her inability to relax? She drove herself hard and expected her employees to follow in her footsteps. Being a woman, she'd known she'd have to work hard to prove to her grandfather that she was executive material, worthy of someday taking her place as head of the family business.

All that work only to find out she'd wasted the past twenty-nine years of her life chasing a goal that wasn't hers to pursue. The futility of it all infuriated her. Leaving her suite, Harper headed to the parking garage where she retrieved her car and headed to the mall for a little shopping therapy.

Harper cruised store after store without buying anything while she pondered how profoundly her life had changed. She had to tell her grandfather the truth, didn't she? Neither Scarlett nor Violet thought it was a good idea. But what toll would living a lie take on her psyche?

Sick of questions that had no easy answers, Harper ducked into a bookstore, deciding what she needed was a few hours of getting lost in someone else's problems. It had been too long since she'd taken time to read something besides reports. She picked up a copy of her favorite author's latest novel and headed to the front to pay.

While she waited behind a mother with two children under the age of five, her attention drifted toward a display of coffee table books. The leopard on the cover of one caught her attention. As a child she'd spent hours flipping through a book of African wildlife photos at her grandmother's home in the Hamptons. She'd found the images riveting and realized now that it was probably what had planted the seeds of longing to travel.

The hair on Harper's arms lifted as she was struck by a sudden realization. Penelope had engaged in an affair with a wildlife photographer. Was it just a coincidence that she'd given Harper's grandmother a book of wildlife photos? Deep in her soul, Harper knew it wasn't.

She stepped out of the checkout line and headed toward the display that had caught her attention. This book wasn't the same as the one in her grandmother's library. Gripped by sudden urgency, she dialed her grandmother's Hamptons house. As expected, Tilly, her grandmother's housekeeper, answered.

"Hi, Tilly, it's Harper."

"Hello, Harper. I'm afraid your grandmother isn't here at the moment."

"Oh, that's right. She mentioned her plans to go shopping when I spoke with her last Sunday." Which was why Harper knew she could call at this time and accomplish her goal without explaining why she was so interested in a book of photographs. "Could you do me a favor?"

"Of course."

"There's a book of African wildlife photos in the library that my mother gave Grandma for her birthday a long time ago. I used to look at it when I visited, but I don't think I've see it since I was thirteen or fourteen. Could you find it for me?"

"Give me a second." If Tilly thought the request was odd, coming out of the blue like this, she gave no sign. The Hamptons house had a five-thousand-square-foot first floor so it took a few minutes before Tilly came back on the line. "I have it here."

Harper exhaled in relief. She'd been half afraid that

the book would have been lost in the past fifteen years. Her grandmother wasn't the most sentimental woman and might not have kept a birthday present from her daughter that long.

"Can you tell me who the photographer was?"

"Greg LeDay."

"Perfect. Thank you, Tilly. And don't mention to anyone that I called. I'll check in with Grandma on Sunday as usual."

"She always loves to hear from you."

Harper ended the call and felt a bit light-headed. Was Greg LeDay her father? With shaking fingers, she tapped his name into the internet browser on her phone and waited impatiently for the search results to come up. To her immense delight he had a website. She went straight to his bio page and spent a long moment staring at the black-and-white photo of a handsome, rugged man in his mid-fifties standing beside a battered jeep, a camera with an enormous lens in his hands. Five giraffes loped across the landscape behind him.

His easy posture and half grin reminded her so much of Ashton that she couldn't breathe for a second. The two men were obviously cut from the same cloth. No wonder she was so drawn to the man who starred in *The Culinary Wanderer.* She had an adventurer's blood running through her veins.

After several minutes of staring at the photo, she began exploring LeDay's website. In addition to being a photographer, he also acted as a guide for others who were interested in taking pictures of wildlife. In fact, he had several tours lined up in the coming months. One left in two days.

An idea bloomed. She emailed LeDay about joining the safari. Abandoning the book she'd come to purchase for a travel guide to South Africa, Harper headed for her car and the nearest sporting goods store. Within ten minutes, she stood before a display of travel bags and finally understood the importance of Ashton's *go* bag. Pack light and be ready to take off for the next exotic location at a moment's notice.

Isn't that what fascinated her about his television show? His lack of baggage, both physical and spiritual? He took what he could comfortably carry. Lightweight clothes that would travel well. His notebooks for when inspiration struck. Some toiletries. And most important? A camera.

Seized by a vision of what she would take on her own adventure, Harper picked out a rolling backpack system and gathered whatever accessories she would need for the next few weeks.

It wasn't until she'd paid for her purchases and lugged them out to her car that she began to question the sanity of what she intended to do. What made her think that this man who might be her father would appreciate her showing up out of the blue? She had no idea if he knew she existed. But if she didn't take the chance and meet him, she might never stop questioning who she was. Her identity secure, she would know whether or not she could stay quiet about her true parentage and spend the rest of her life living a lie. Scarlett and Violet had already promised to support whatever decision she made. She was lucky to have them in her life.

Anticipation filled her with a wild sort of joy as she returned to her hotel suite and sifted through all she'd bought. It was a ridiculous amount, she realized, staring at it scattered over her bed. Never before had she needed to mull over every ounce of what she was packing. Her trips had involved porters, bellhops and hired cars.

Harper abandoned her packing conundrum and went online to check flights to Johannesburg, South Africa. To her surprise she had several choices all leaving that evening. Why wait? Now that she'd made the decision to go, every minute that went by increased her craving to be off.

Unable to believe how easy the whole thing was, she assembled her own *go* bag. Small enough to fit in an over-head bin, it weighed thirty pounds completely loaded. By the time she'd dressed in jeans, a white T-shirt and a brown leather bomber jacket she'd found in the back of her closet, her nerves were humming with excitement.

As she turned off the lights and pulled the door of her suite shut behind her, Harper was struck by a profound sense of stepping across the threshold into a whole new state of being. It was thrilling to be rushing off into the night with no idea what to anticipate next and no way of controlling the outcome.

She was halfway down the hall when the elevator door opened and Ashton emerged pulling his own *go* bag behind him. When he spotted her, he stopped dead. His position in the doorway kept the elevator open.

"Where are you going?" he demanded as she stepped onto the elevator beside him.

"I could ask you the same thing." Disappointment hit her. She needed him in Las Vegas, focused on the soon-to-open restaurant.

"I was coming to see you."

She glanced pointedly at his luggage. "And after that?"

"I'm flying to New York for a few days. The negotiations for the new show have reached a critical point."

"How critical?"

"I may be on the verge of losing the deal."

Hope flared. If he didn't do the new show he could stay on with *The Culinary Wanderer*. She was careful to keep her voice neutral as she said, "Maybe that's not the worst that could happen."

"But doing the new show means I'll get to spend most of the year in New York City."

Where she would be if she stopped asking questions about her biological father and accepted that she belonged in charge of Fontaine Hotels and Resorts. Would her relationship with Ashton develop into something serious if they were both in New York?

"It sounds like an amazing opportunity," she told him. "I just wish you could do both the new show and *The Culinary Wanderer.*"

"Sounds like you don't want me around." He said it with a wry kick of his lips, but his eyes were serious as he awaited her response.

She'd felt connected to him these past few days. He'd filled her head with his stories and inspired her to go in search of a few of her own.

"It isn't that." She paused, unsure if she should voice how much she craved his company. The man had one foot out the door on the best of days. "Are you sure you're going to be happy if you're stuck in one place for a long time? Won't you get bored?"

"If you're worried about my ability to control my need for change, don't be. Once I find something I love, I have no trouble sticking with it."

"And yet here you are leaving town a week and a half before Batouri is set to open."

His lips tightened momentarily. "Everything is handled. I've given Dae my recipes and instructions and he knows how I work. He can keep things on track until Cole gets here. And I'll be back in a few days."

"It's your restaurant. Your reputation on the line." From his expression she could tell he hadn't expected her to pass complete control of the project to him. "I'm sure you know what you're doing."

"Which brings us to you. If you're heading to New York, I can give you a ride in the network's corporate jet."

"Thank you, but I've already booked my flight."

"Wouldn't you rather travel in style? I can promise the pantry is well stocked."

"It's kind of you to offer, but we are destined for different locations."

He scrutinized her clothes and her bag. "Where are you going?"

"South Africa."

Ashton didn't know what to make of her answer. Two nights earlier they'd enjoyed a playful evening of food and wine. Last night they'd made love. She'd never once made mention of an upcoming trip much less one to Africa. Maybe he wasn't the only one keeping secrets.

The elevator doors opened, and Harper stepped forward with purpose and energy. Ashton followed. Since they were both heading to the airport, he'd have a good twenty minutes to get to the core of what was going on.

He eyed her suitcase. It was the size he'd expect a woman to take for a long weekend. "How long are you planning to be gone?"

"I don't know. A week. Maybe two. It depends." She trailed off.

Not normally one to pick up on the nuances of other people's emotional states, Ashton found that when it came to Harper, he'd become hyperaware of her moods. Something was up and he wasn't going to let her go until he knew what it was.

"I didn't realize Fontaine had expanded into Africa."

"It hasn't."

"Then you're scouting locations?"

"No."

Her short answers were creating more confusion than understanding. Harper was many things. Goal oriented, resourceful, outspoken. Never evasive.

Ashton used his height and weight advantage to herd her away from the line of taxis. She was not escaping from him until he was satisfied he knew the whole story. "I have a car waiting."

"I can take a cab."

"You can also accept a ride."

"Thank you." But there was very little gratitude in her tone. She wanted to go her own way. It made him all that much more determined to not let her.

After giving instructions to the driver where to drop Harper off, he waited until their luggage was stowed in the trunk and the town car was navigating East Flamingo Road before he continued his interrogation. "Is this trip business or pleasure?"

"Why are you so curious?"

"Because I would think with Batouri set to open in less than two weeks you might have mentioned an impending trip out of the country."

"It came up rather fast."

"How fast?"

"This afternoon."

The traffic was flowing more smoothly than usual down Paradise Road. The short ride to the airport, which usually took twenty minutes, was going to take closer to ten. Ashton was running out of time to get the answers he wanted.

"What the hell is going on with you, Harper? This isn't like you at all."

Her brown eyes were fierce as she met his gaze. "I'm not sure that's true."

"You've lost me."

"Since I was eleven I've had a plan for how my life was going to go. I set goals and achieved them, all with one target in mind."

"Running Fontaine Hotels and Resorts."

She nodded. "But what no one knows is how often I've wondered what it would be like to give it all up and run away. To pack a bag and see the world, not from the back of a taxi, but on the back of a motorcycle or in an open jeep or even on a camel."

Passion drenched her tone. Her longing made his heart contract. He recognized what it felt like to yearn, even though he'd long ago come to terms with the futility of craving what could never be. He'd promised himself to never be that weak again, but his developing connection with Harper sparked a long-buried emotion. Hope.

"What does all this have to do with your trip to South Africa?"

"I realize it's all been in vain."

Harper's hand had been hovering near the door handle since the car had entered the airport limits. As soon as the vehicle came to a complete stop, she was out the door. The driver popped the trunk, and Harper had her bag on the curb before Ashton even exited the car. Despite her haste, he moved quickly enough to block her path into the terminal.

"My flight leaves in ninety minutes. I have to get through security."

"Then you don't have a lot of time to waste. Why are you going to Africa?"

"I have something I need to take care of."

"Such as?" He crossed his arms over his chest and regarded her as if he had all the time in the world to wait for her answer.

She blew out a breath. "Some complicated family business."

"Hotel business?"

"Personal business."

"And you don't feel like sharing?"

"Maybe when I get back."

"Talk to me, Harper." Ashton was more than a little disturbed to feel her slipping away from him. "I told you things no one else knows."

Her gaze pleaded with him to let her go, but he held firm and at last she caved. "Fine. I'm going to find a man who might be my father."

"I thought your father was dead."

She paused a beat before answering. "The man I thought was my father is dead. I think my real father is a wildlife photographer who leads photography safaris throughout Africa." She sounded completely composed as if this was old news, but the tension around her mouth betrayed that all was not well.

It all came together in a heartbeat. "So you're not a Fontaine?"

"It appears I'm not."

"And finding this out has led to the questions you've been having about the decisions you've made in your career?"

"I'm not a Fontaine." Agony fractured her voice. "I have no right to be CEO."

"You have worked toward this all your life."

"My grandfather wants one of his granddaughters to take over the company."

"And you think he will reject you after twenty-nine years because you're not biologically related? Could anyone be that heartless?"

"You don't understand how important family is to my grandfather. After my father..." She grimaced. "After my father died and Grandfather discovered he had other granddaughters, he came up with his contest to determine who was best qualified to run the company." She dashed away a tear from the corner of her eye and rushed on. "It was my birthright. My dream. I'd dedicated my life to proving I deserved to be CEO one day, and he expected me to prove it all over again."

Horns honked behind him as cars jockeyed for space at the curb. Departing passengers hurried past. A police officer, directing traffic, blew his whistle. The chaos pressed against Ashton's back, but he braced himself and focused completely on Harper.

Four words summed up everything he felt for her. "How can I help?"

He put out a hand, offering comfort and support, but she backed away.

"You can't." She gave her head a vehement shake.

Despite being stung by her rejection, he persisted. "Where in South Africa are you heading?"

"Pretoria."

"Where are you staying?"

"I haven't decided." It wasn't like her to be so unprepared.

"I have a friend at the Pretoria Capital Hotel. Ask for Giles Dumas. He's the executive chef for their restaurant."

"Thank you." Gratitude softened her lips into a smile for a second. "I have to go. I can't miss my flight."

Staying put and letting her walk away from him was the hardest thing he'd done in a long time. When she disappeared through the sliding glass doors of the terminal, Ashton slid into the back of the town car and focused his attention on the traffic visible through the windshield.

She had her path to follow. He had his. If only he could shake his thoughts free of her. He had his own problems to worry about. The network folks would expect him to make a strong showing during his taping. He needed to be completely focused to impress them.

Eight

With the first and shortest leg of her long journey behind her, Harper fastened her seat belt and stared out the window with dry, scratchy eyes. By flying business class, she'd saved eight thousand dollars on her ticket, but she'd found herself incapable of sleeping sitting up during the nearly ten-hour flight to London. Nor had she been able to nod off during her five-hour layover. Pair that with her sleepless night the previous evening and Harper estimated she'd been awake around forty-eight hours.

At least on the leg between London and Johannesburg she wasn't stuck in a middle seat. She propped a pillow between her head and the wall of the cabin and let out a huge breath as a wave of exhaustion flowed over her. She fell asleep not long after the plane stopped climbing.

The popping of her ears woke her as the plane reduced altitude. She checked the seat back monitor that kept track of the distance traveled and saw that they were a little over an hour from touching down in South Africa. Her pulse jumped. She was about to land in a foreign country and go in search of a man she hadn't known existed two days earlier. The town where he lived was a forty-five minute drive from Johannesburg and she had yet to receive a response to her email requesting information on the seven-day safari he was leading the day after she arrived.

She thought it might be a good idea to get to know him a little before announcing that she'd traveled halfway around the world to see if she was his daughter.

From his bio she knew that he'd never been married. Dedicating his life to his passion for Africa, he'd won several prestigious awards and had his work published in more than two dozen magazines. For the past day and a half she'd tried to find herself in this man she shared genes with. They shared a focus on their work and a determination to achieve greatness, but when it came to their careers, Greg LeDay had more in common with Ashton than her.

Both men were creative geniuses. LeDay's photography was brilliant in the same way Ashton's culinary masterpieces won him notoriety.

By comparison, what had she done? She'd worked hard and had nothing she was proud to display as her body of work. Her passion involved planning, organizing and making things happen. She was good at telling people what to do, being ruthless. How many of her employees called her a bitch behind her back?

Harper wasn't feeling all that organized or ruthless at the moment. She was drifting on a sea of uncertainty. Impatient with herself, she pulled out her phone and logged on to the plane's Wi-Fi network. It was time to reconnect with her organized self. She hadn't yet planned her trip beyond booking her flight to Johannesburg. She needed to figure out how she was going to get to Pretoria and where she was going to stay once she got there.

To her delight, the two cities were linked by a high-speed train line that she could pick up at the airport. She would have to change trains, but after doing so she would arrive in Pretoria in less than half an hour. Harper then turned her attention to finding the hotel Ashton had suggested and booked a room for two nights. By the time the plane's doors opened to allow the passengers to disembark, she was feeling completely in charge once more.

Finding the train was easy. She'd exchanged dollars for rand along the way and arrived at the platform just as the train was pulling in. As adventures went, this trip was feeling awfully mundane. She stepped onto the train, secured her bag and settled into a clean, comfortable seat by the window. Despite getting sleep on the plane, the train's rocking motion made it difficult to keep her eyes open. She fought the pull. The distance between the stations wasn't great and she could miss her exchange if she wasn't careful.

As it was, she wasn't fully awake when the train pulled into Marlboro station. Yawning wearily, she got to her feet and waited for an opening in the crowd of exiting passengers so she could step into the aisle and collect her bag. Something hard clipped her temple, knocking her sideways. Stunned by the blow, on the verge of losing consciousness, she didn't fight the hands that shoved her into the seat and stripped away the bag that held her cash and passport.

Before her head cleared, her assailant was long gone and the last of the passengers had disembarked. Harper staggered to her feet, but before she could reach her luggage, the door closed and the train moved forward. The pain in her head made Harper's thoughts thick and sluggish. She dropped into the closest empty seat and closed her eyes. What was she supposed to do now?

Ashton stepped out of a cab on the corner of Ninth Avenue and Twenty-eighth Street in Chelsea and saw his old friend Craig Turner waiting for him by the curb. Since the Lifestyle people weren't expecting him until two that afternoon, Ashton had decided to check in with his old mentor and wasn't surprised to learn that Craig was still volunteering at Holy Apostles Soup Kitchen.

"Ashton, good to see you." The sixty-five-year-old restaurateur wrapped Ashton in a tight bear hug. "You're looking wonderful. Television suits you."

"It has its moments."

When Ashton had first come to New York before landing his first television series, he'd spent two years in Craig's kitchen learning everything there was to know about what it took to run a successful restaurant. He'd gleaned a lot. And yet, with four restaurants under his belt, Ashton knew he still had plenty of Craig's wisdom left to absorb.

"And now you're stepping into the big time with a show here in New York."

It shouldn't have astonished him that Craig knew this; little happened in New York having to do with food that Craig missed. "We'll see. Nothing's finalized yet."

"And your restaurant in Las Vegas. That's set to open next week. Things going okay?"

"I'll tell you in a couple weeks."

Craig laughed heartily. "I'm glad you could meet me here."

"No problem."

"Once a week I come down to volunteer. For two hours every day they serve a hot meal to over a thousand people. Makes me feel good to give back."

"Of course." Ashton smiled, but as soon as he entered the busy church, he felt his muscles tense as long-forgotten memories of the dinners his parents had organized for the locals resurfaced.

As a kid he'd resented the hours of free time he'd lost helping his mother fix and serve the meals while his father practiced his ministry on the captive audience. Now, as he put on an apron and rolled up his sleeves, he recalled the day when his outlook had changed—when a loathsome chore had become an opportunity to create something amazing in the kitchen. But for a long time after he'd left home and joined up with Chapman's gang, he'd equated his love for cooking with surrendering to his parents' insistence that he become more like them.

He fell into the rhythm of serving as if twenty years hadn't passed. Looking back on those days, he could recall his resentment and frustration, but lacked empathy for his younger self. Seeing the gratitude in the eyes of those who moved past him now, Ashton recalled how many people his parents had been able to help.

So maybe he'd been too hard on his mother and father all these years. But he still wasn't able to excuse his father's insistence that everyone should believe the same things he did. His disregard for any opinion that wasn't his had put father and son at odds too many times. If his father had listened to him once or twice, maybe Ashton would have felt valued and wouldn't have left. He'd never know.

Several hours later, Ashton waved off the thanks from the volunteer leaders and followed Craig outside. It might not have been how he'd chosen to spend the morning, but it had given him some fodder for thought.

"Thanks for the help. Can I drop you somewhere?"

Ashton shook his head. "I'm going to walk a bit."

"It was good seeing you. Perhaps when your new series gets rolling you can come have dinner with me."

"I'd like that."

The two men parted ways and Ashton strode down the street as if he had someplace to be, when in truth, he was just trying to escape the pressure inside himself.

He'd not yet heard anything from Giles. Given that Harper's flight time was a little over twenty-six hours and the time difference between New York and Johannesburg was seven hours, he imagined she should be arriving in Pretoria around one in the morning New York time, depending on her stops and layovers. Being out of touch with her bothered him. He craved the sound of her voice and longed to share with her his revelations while serving at the soup kitchen.

Something about her invited him to confide his secrets. He wasn't sure why he'd told her about his parents or how he'd left home. Disclosing his past wasn't something he did. He wasn't sure why he didn't want anyone to know that he was the son of missionaries or that he'd left home at an early age. Maybe it was the mess he'd been involved in when he left home that he was ashamed of. What he'd been forced to do. The darkness he'd faced in his soul.

He reflected on his decision to keep those things hidden. Who was he really protecting? If Harper had an inkling of what he held back, she would dig until she unearthed the truth. Would she turn away in disgust or understand? She'd grown up in a cocoon of wealth and polite society. Instinct told him she'd be appalled to learn what he'd done while living with Chapman's gang.

They were so different. She, all bossy businesswoman, planning every little thing to death. He, the go-getter, leaping before looking because what fun was life without a little danger? She conquered. He explored. Very different philosophies.

That they'd been able to work together these past nine months without driving each other mad continued to baffle him. Maybe it worked because they were good for each other. He needed her planning capabilities to keep him in check. And he knew his adventurous side had rubbed off on her. Why else would she have hopped on a plane to South Africa?

Harper gripped the armrest as the train sped through the flat landscape dotted with buildings. She was traveling in the wrong direction. How far out of her way had she gone? Almost as soon as the question surfaced, the train began to slow down. She was on her feet, her luggage in her hand by the time the doors opened.

No longer able to assume the people around her were innocuous fellow travelers, Harper regarded everyone who drew near her as a potential threat. When no one in her vicinity seemed at all interested in her, she took a seat on a nearby bench and took stock of her situation.

Her cash and passport were gone. She still had her rail pass and the credit card she'd used to purchase it tucked in her back pocket. Her phone had been in her hand at the time of the attack and she'd managed to keep ahold of it. And she had her luggage. All was not lost. She would get on the train to Pretoria and catch a cab to the American Embassy there.

All she needed was her birth certificate and the extra photo…which she kept in the luggage she'd left behind in Las Vegas. Anxiety swelled once more. Without identification how was she supposed to prove who she was?

Frozen and unable to function, Harper stared at her hands. She was far from home and quite alone. Not to mention her head ached and panic was jumbling her thoughts. The ebb and flow of train passengers caused her suspicion to spike.

By fits and starts her brain began to function again. She needed to figure out which train traveled north so she could get back on track. The Gautrain's schedule was still in her internet browser. She located the route map and discovered she wasn't in as bad a shape as she thought. The train to Pretoria passed through this station, as well. She just needed to find the correct track.

Fifteen minutes later, Harper collapsed into her seat on the Pretoria-bound train and patted herself on the back. With the shock of being robbed fading, she was better able to function. During the journey north she pinned the American Embassy on her map app and located the hotel, as well.

Her stomach growled, reminding her she hadn't eaten anything since her stopover in London. She would worry about that later. She had to secure a home base where Mary could send her documents. Once she had those in hand, she could go to the embassy. Ashton had told her to ask for his friend. Perhaps that would be enough to enable her to check in without her passport. She crossed her fingers and hoped.

An hour after stepping onto the platform in Pretoria station and taking a taxi to the hotel, Harper launched into her story of being mugged for the third time. Hunger and frustration were draining what few reserves she had left.

"No, I didn't file a report with the police. I didn't know where to find a police station. I just wanted to get here and register."

"But we can't do that without you having documentation," the manager in charge of the front desk explained. "Don't you have a copy of your passport page to show us?"

"As I've already told your staff, the decision to visit Pretoria was a last-minute thing and I left all my backup documentation behind. My assistant is going to overnight it to me, but I need to have a place she can send it."

"She can't send it here unless you're registered."

Harper closed her eyes and sucked in a huge breath. "Giles." She'd forgotten about him. "I was supposed to ask for Giles…" His last name eluded her. "I believe he's the executive chef here?"

The manager regarded her solemnly. "He is our executive chef."

"Would he be around? I was told to come here and to say that Ashton Croft sent me."

"We'll call the kitchen. Perhaps you should take a seat over there and we'll see if he has time to speak to you."

It wasn't the most promising offer, but at this point Harper was ready to take what she could get. "I'm quite hungry. Tell him I'll be in the restaurant."

She followed the hostess toward a table on the patio and sank into the plastic chair with a grateful sigh. A smiling waitress came almost immediately to take her order. The dinner menu had so many delicious items on it she had trouble choosing. In the end she settled on game picatta because the description made her mouth water. Tender slices of game pan fried with button mushrooms, mixed peppercorns, doused with sweet Marsala and bound with cream, served on fettuccine dusted with Parmesan cheese.

It arrived at her table, delivered by a tall, handsome man with salt-and-pepper hair and a dashing goatee. She glanced from his face to his chef whites without comprehension as he set the plate before her.

"You're Harper Fontaine?"

At his recognition tears began streaming down her face. She nodded, too overcome by relief to speak.

"My name is Giles Dumas. I understand you ran into a little trouble getting here." He smiled gently as she nodded a second time. "Our mutual friend will be very glad to hear you've arrived. Now, what can I do to help?"

Nine

Gut tight with foreboding, Ashton stood with his back to the conference table and stared out over the Manhattan skyline. Behind him two of the network guys were speaking with Vince. The taping hadn't gone as well as he would have liked. Since dropping Harper off at the airport he'd been edgy and distracted. Nor could he be certain that she'd taken his advice and booked a room at the Pretoria Capital Hotel until he heard from his buddy Giles.

He told himself just because he enjoyed venturing off the beaten track didn't mean she would be foolish enough to go somewhere she could get into trouble. But until he knew she was safe, Ashton wouldn't be able to shake the sensation that he'd made a mistake letting her go by herself halfway around the world to find a father she'd never met. Even after she shoved his offer of help back at him he couldn't get her out of his head. He was worried about her emotional state and the fact that she was a woman unused to traveling alone.

Vince came to stand beside him. His manager's lack of chatter felt as ominous as the clouds above the city.

Ashton broke the silence. "They weren't wowed by my audition tape."

"It wasn't quite what they were expecting," Vince agreed. "Some aspects of it went over great, others they'd like to work on with you."

"And?" Ashton prompted, hearing the low note in Vince's voice and guessing there was more bad news.

"It's just this little thing about your image. You've been the bad boy of travel adventures, eating exotic cuisine, meeting the natives."

The description was a little off-putting, but Ashton figured Vince was offering his own spin on what the producers had said.

"How do they want my image to change?"

"They're thinking lose the jeans and leather jacket and put you into chef whites. But mostly…" Vince hesitated. "They want you to cut your hair so that you'll look more… polished."

It wasn't an outrageous demand, but Ashton wasn't sure he wanted to look like something he wasn't. And yet, wasn't the whole point of doing this cooking show so he could change things up in his career? "Anything else?"

Vince looked relieved that Ashton's temper hadn't blown up. "They're wondering if you can stay in New York a few more days."

He needed to get back to Las Vegas and Batouri. Even though Dae was sending him frequent updates that things were running smoothly, it was a week and a half before the restaurant opened. And as Harper had repeatedly pointed out, Batouri was his responsibility.

"Ash?" Vince prompted. "What should I tell them?"

Harper had accused him of putting his television career before Batouri, but hadn't he also put it before her? So what if they barely knew each other? Ashton couldn't shake the notion that she needed him and he'd let her down.

"Tell them no."

"Have you lost your mind? You can't say no after quitting *The Culinary Wanderer.* What if they find someone else? What are you going to do then?"

Vince seemed to have forgotten that with several restaurants in various countries, Ashton wasn't dependent on the money he made doing television shows. He just enjoyed the celebrity and the experiences he'd had over the years.

"Write a cookbook." With the help of a very special woman who was at a crossroads of her own.

"A cookbook? Have you lost your mind? Lifestyle Network is going to make you famous."

"They've left me hanging for four months. Now they're demanding I drop everything at a moment's notice?" Ashton's frustration spilled over. "They're going to have to wait."

"I'm not sure they'll like that answer." Vince's eyes shifted toward the group of executives. "They could go with someone else."

Ashton mentally cursed. This was his project. They'd strung him along and now they were threatening to replace him?

"Let them," he snarled. "Whatever they do with the show, it's not going to be a success without me." His gaze collided with Vince's.

"Okay." But his manager didn't look happy. "You're the star. We walk away from this deal." Vince assessed Ashton's expression and shed his doubts with a nod. "Once word gets out you'll be hit with a dozen offers before the week's out."

Ashton wasn't sure his manager was right, but he was confident something bigger and better was just around the next curve. In the meantime he would see to Batouri's grand opening and spend some time getting to know more about Harper Fontaine.

As his thoughts returned to her, all optimism drained away. Why couldn't he shake the notion that he should travel to Africa to be with her? The thought was ridiculous. She'd insisted he focus his full attention on Batouri. He'd incur her fury if he did anything as idiotic as leave the country mere days before its opening.

"I need to get to the airport," Ashton announced. "Let me know what the outcome of the meeting is."

"Are you heading back to Las Vegas now?"

"Not yet."

"Where then?"

"Pretoria."

Vince looked utterly baffled. "Where?"

"South Africa."

Harper's second day in South Africa had gone much more smoothly than her first. Before going to bed the night before, she'd contacted Mary and arranged to have her backup documentation shipped to the hotel. Then, with nothing to do but wait, she took the opportunity to sleep late and get her bearings.

Now, bathed in early afternoon sunshine, Harper was enjoying a glass of wine in a corner of the patio. A shadow fell across her South African tour book. Thinking it was her waitress she looked up. Ashton stood beside her chair looking every inch a dashing world traveler in jeans and a pale blue button-down shirt with the sleeves rolled up to expose the long faint scars on his forearms. With one hand he held a black leather jacket over his shoulder and the other rested on the handle of his *go* bag.

Heart jumping wildly, Harper was too stunned to answer the come-and-get-me call of his lopsided grin. "What are you doing here?"

"I decided someone needed to chronicle your first adventure, so here I am." He pulled out the chair beside hers and settled into it.

"I thought you had a meeting in New York."

"It was over sooner than I expected so I hopped on a plane and here I am."

He didn't elaborate, and she wondered how things had gone.

"My trip took over twenty-six hours. How did you get here so fast?"

"Direct flights from JFK only take fifteen hours." He settled into the chair across from hers. "What are you drinking?"

"Something local. It's quite good." Her brain still wasn't functioning properly. She continued to stare at him in amazement. With his arrival, being in South Africa had taken on a whole new joy. "Shouldn't you be in Las Vegas preparing for Batouri's opening?"

"I spoke with Cole an hour ago. He arrived in Vegas and has everything running smoothly. Tell me about your visit so far."

Concern for what might be going wrong with the opening buzzed in the back of her mind, but she'd made the decision to abandon her post at this critical time and had to trust that Ashton knew what he was doing, too. "You called Giles to tell him I was coming. How did you know I would?"

"Since you usually have everything planned to the second and hadn't yet booked a hotel, I knew you'd be open to my recommendation." He paused a beat. "And you trust me."

The knowing glint in his gaze made her cross. Harper picked up her wine and took a sip. "Your meeting in New York must have gone your way for you to be here right now."

"Actually, it went rather poorly." He signaled the waitress. "They want me to cut my hair. I told them to go to hell."

While he ordered wine for himself and a melted cheese bowl appetizer, Harper narrowed her eyes and tried to picture him without his wayward, sun-streaked locks. With his dimples and sparkling blue eyes it didn't really matter what the producers did to try and make him look more civilized. In his heart, he was always going to be a reckless adventurer. That they were trying to change him was idiotic. Didn't they understand that was the basis of his charm?

"And instead of returning to Las Vegas where your restaurant is opening in a week you decided to come here?" Did he expect her to be glad to see him? Which she was.

"I didn't think you were ready to fly solo."

"You think I need a babysitter."

He radiated innocence. "Did I say that?"

"You've spoken with Giles."

"He called me before my flight left."

"He told you, didn't he?"

"Told me what?"

She didn't believe his casualness for a second. "That I was mugged on the train." When he didn't react with shock and concern, she knew her suspicions had been right. "I suppose you think I was foolish for coming here alone."

"Not at all. This is a very safe country for tourists. The same thing could have happened to you in New York or Las Vegas. I'm sorry you were attacked and I'm angry with myself for not coming with you."

His words stirred up the emotional tornado she'd been caught in all week. A tear formed in the corner of her eye. She dashed it away. "You had important things to do."

"None of them are more important than you."

It was a huge admission for her to hear, and she wondered how he'd react if she told him that she was falling in love with him. Better not. She was feeling too vulnerable and he'd already confessed that he didn't want her depending on him. If she harnessed him with the burden of her growing attachment, he might turn right around and get back on a plane. And she very badly needed him. She'd just have to keep letting him think she didn't.

"Because you aren't free to pursue another project until Batouri is opened and I'm satisfied that your end of our arrangement is complete?" It hurt to see shadows overcome the bright blue of his gaze.

His wine arrived at the same time as the food, interrupting the silence that hung between them. Harper focused on putting the goat cheese and roasted tomato bruschetta mixture on a slice of toasted baguette.

"When are you planning on going to the embassy about getting a new passport?"

"My assistant overnighted my documents. I'll go when they get here."

"And in the meantime? Have you had any luck locating the man you believe is your father?"

"His name is Greg LeDay. He left this morning for Kruger National Park. The safari he's leading was booked and I couldn't get in. He won't be back in town for ten days. I can't wait around that long." She gave him a sheepish smile. "Seems my first impulsive adventure is a complete disaster."

"Adventure is immune to disaster." Ashton pointed at her with the knife he'd been using to smooth cheese on his bread. "There may be setbacks and detours, but often those are what send you in a new and exciting direction."

His optimism was contagious. "See, this is why I'm such a fan." She couldn't help but be drawn in by his enthusiasm. "You have a knack for transforming the challenges into opportunities."

"Words to put on my tombstone."

"It's a lot better than what they'd inscribe on mine. 'She planned every second of her life to death.'"

Ashton coughed long and hard until tears ran from his eyes.

"Are you okay?" she asked him as the fit slowly abated.

"I inhaled some of my wine. That was some pretty dark humor just now," he said. "It caught me by surprise."

"Did it?" She considered what she'd said. "I guess I think that way fairly often, but it rarely comes out. It's not the sort of thing my mother appreciated hearing so I learned to bottle it up."

"There are more layers to you than anyone realizes, aren't there?"

Harper shrugged. The admiration in his gaze was both thrilling and a touch uncomfortable. She'd concentrated on doing and saying the right thing her whole life. It was liberating to let loose, but it worried her a little how unmanageable her impulses might become.

It wasn't until after a second round of wine, when Ashton glanced at his watch, that Harper realized the shadows had lengthened. Once again she noticed how in his entertaining company time seemed to fly.

"I'm going to shower and then take you out for a terrific dinner."

"Have you registered?"

"Not yet." He rose and went to where he'd stashed his *go* bag by a large planter.

"Why don't you use my shower then?"

He turned and looked at her, his eyes searching her face.

"We both know how tonight will end up. Why pay for two rooms?"

"That's rather presumptuous of you."

Despite the cooling air, her skin heated. She got to her feet, hoping to appear more confident than she felt. "I'm just being realistic."

Ashton wrapped his arm around her waist and kissed

her, his lips warm and sweetly persuasive. "Have I mentioned how much I appreciate your practical nature?"

Relaxing against his solid body, Harper gave in to a satisfied smile. "You can after dinner."

"How about a little before and a lot after?"

"That sounds quite acceptable."

A sliver of sunlight lanced through a narrow gap between the closed curtains, waking Ashton. From the angle, he surmised it was early afternoon. Jumping multiple time zones had always been a part of his life and from an early age he'd adapted to functioning on less sleep than the average person, but combine his long trip with an insatiable Harper Fontaine and it was amazing he hadn't slept until dusk.

He rolled onto his back and stretched his arm across the empty mattress. It was cool to the touch. She'd been gone some time. He couldn't blame her. From the heaviness of his limbs he'd probably been sleeping like the dead. Some fun traveling companion he was.

A tented piece of paper sat on her pillow. He read her note and grimaced. She'd gone to the embassy to see about her passport. That meant she wouldn't return anytime soon.

Ashton pushed upright and ran his fingers through his hair. He'd use the time to make some arrangements. Last night as they'd talked over dinner, it came to him that no matter how short her trip was, she really shouldn't leave South Africa without seeing a little of its natural beauty.

It took him an hour's worth of phone calls to get everything in place. When she arrived half an hour later, looking jubilant and proud of herself, he wrapped her in a warm embrace.

"How'd it go at the embassy?"

"They scolded me for not filing a police report, but I should have a temporary passport early afternoon tomorrow."

"That's good news. And I have some, as well." He drew her toward the hotel room door. "Let's get something to eat and I'll tell you all about it."

This time he took her to a restaurant with unassuming furnishings and mouthwatering aromas emanating from the long buffet. They filled their plates with authentic South African dishes and returned to their table. As they ate, Ashton did his best to explain all the things they'd chosen. It had been over ten years since he'd last visited South Africa and some of the more exotic fare wasn't familiar.

As he chewed a bite of crocodile, he wondered if maybe the producers of *The Culinary Wanderer* had been right about coming to Africa for this next season. He'd blocked out just how diverse and delicious the cuisine was.

"Tell me your news."

"I found your father."

"But I'd already done that."

"Yes, but I know where he is right now."

"How?"

"You forget how well-connected I am." He saluted himself with his wineglass before continuing. "A guy I knew knew another guy who has used your father to gather wildlife footage in the past and had his phone number. Turns out he's not far from here. I wasn't able to get us into the camp where he's staying, but there's a lodge about an hour away that a friend of mine owns."

Harper had stopped eating and was looking a little shell-shocked. "When?"

"Late tomorrow after you get your passport. I chartered a plane to take us into Nelspruit where we'll pick up a car and drive to Kruger National Park. It shouldn't take more than a couple hours. We can catch up with him before he heads out the following day."

What he really needed to do was get on a plane and go back to Las Vegas, but she couldn't bring herself to remind him that his first priority should be Batouri.

"I don't know what to say." Her voice wavered. "I'd pre-pared myself to leave without even meeting him. Thank you."

"No thanks required."

Her gaze locked on his face. "Well, I won't take it back."

Warmth spread from his chest through his whole body. He reached for her hand and smiled as she slipped her fingers through his. The couple sitting at the table beside them smiled. Ashton imagined the romantic picture he and Harper made. In the past while he'd never kept his personal life hidden, he hadn't indulged in public displays of affection, either. With Harper he wanted the whole world to notice that she belonged with him.

He'd even started thinking in terms of guiding her to all the places he'd visited and loved. Her ambivalence about her future was a perfect opening to present all the possibilities they could explore together.

By two the next day, Harper's temporary passport was ready to pick up. They headed straight for the airport where they were met by their flight's copilot and escorted onto a well-maintained eight-passenger plane.

As the sun was approaching the horizon almost three hours later, Ashton was braking to a halt alongside a Range Rover of similar age to their own at the Grant Tented Camp. Scattered along the river were six luxurious tents with king-size beds, en suite bathrooms and private terraces. Tucked among thick stands of mature trees and connected by a raised wooden walkway, each tent enjoyed a great deal of privacy.

"Why don't you have a look around while I get us checked in."

Harper opened her door and stepped out, a look of awe on her face. "This isn't exactly what I pictured when you told me we were going to spend a couple nights in a tent camp."

He patted the roof of the Range Rover. "It's not exactly a

camel." He gestured around them. "And it's not exactly the desert, although we are close to the end of the dry season. But at least there are tents. I hope you enjoy it."

She was touched that he'd gone to so much trouble to make her quest to South Africa such a marvelous experience. "Of course I will. How could I not?"

She accompanied him into the tented, open-air lounge and wandered toward the small pool nestled against the deck that overlooked the river. Built of local rock and surrounded by lush plants, it seemed like a completely natural addition to the landscape. Ashton went to see about their accommodations, and Harper wandered until she found the small dining room, also tented, with tables set with white cloth, china and crystal, mahogany chairs and candelabras awaiting the touch of a match.

Such elegance tucked into a wild, untamed landscape charmed Harper. Had Ashton guessed the place was so romantic? She was almost dizzy in anticipation of seeing where they would sleep as she went back to the lounge to await Ashton's return.

The dozen or so guests she noticed scattered about spoke in low voices as if not wanting to disturb the peacefulness of such a tranquil spot. Harper hadn't been here more than ten minutes and she was as relaxed as if she'd been hypnotized by a master.

"Ready?" Ashton's low voice rumbled behind her.

She turned and willingly accepted the hand he held out to her. "I love it here."

"I'm glad."

They walked down a path bordered by hanging lanterns that wound through the vegetation behind the cottages. When they reached the last one, Ashton unlocked the door and pushed it open. Harper took a few steps inside and hesitated in the dimness until Ashton located a light switch.

She gasped in delight.

The tent fabric was held up by a pole in the middle of

the large space, forming a fifteen-foot-high ceiling. There was a king-size bed with white bedding, a walnut wardrobe with glass doors and a chandelier suspended overhead, and a sitting area that held a couch flanked by two chairs and a fireplace. Golden light spilled from an assortment of lamps both attached to the olive-green walls and scattered on the various small tables. A bottle of champagne was cooling in a wine bucket on the colonial-style coffee table.

Kicking off her sandals, she curled her toes into the thick area rug that covered the tent's wood floor. After a slow spin to catalog their accommodations, she pulled Ashton toward her and dazzled him with a long, sexy kiss. "I've been in five-star hotels that weren't as nice as this," she murmured, leaning her cheek against his heaving chest. "It's the most perfect place I've ever seen."

"I'm glad you approve."

A knock sounded on the screen door. Ashton's arms tightened around her briefly before he went to answer. It was a porter. He deposited their luggage inside the door and showed them the canvas flaps they could roll down over the wall of screen windows if the night grew too chilly. When he left, Harper turned to Ashton with a predatory smile and backed him up to the couch.

He ripped his navy Henley shirt over his head while her fingers plucked his belt loose and released the button that held his waistband closed. As she unzipped his pants, she used her free hand to shove him onto the couch. He landed with a soft bounce, and she climbed onto his lap, her knees sinking into the pale gold cushions on either side of his thighs.

With her fingers tangled in his hair, she sought his mouth with hers in an open, wet kiss that left no doubt about her intentions. He gave her all the passion she demanded, groaning deep in his chest as she rocked against his swollen erection, the brief contact satisfying neither of them. Her fingers stroked over his skin in hot, frantic movements. The feel of him brushing against where she needed him the most shot a bolt of the purest frustration through her.

Her hunger communicated itself to Ashton. He stripped off her T-shirt and popped the clasp of her bra, tossing both aside with a ragged exhale. Then his fingers cupped her bare breasts, kneading evocatively until her nipples pebbled against his palms. The thrumming in her blood grew more urgent.

She sucked on his lip and let his breath fill her. A growl greeted her ears as she eased her hand between their bodies and lifted him free of his confining clothes. Smiling, she nipped his neck and at the same time grasped his erection firmly and stroked from base to tip before putting her mouth down over him. His hips bucked. He let out a startled curse, and she chuckled.

"Damn." He had no more words.

His head fell back against the cushion as she continued her slow, steady strokes. When she felt she had him completely beneath her spell, she slid his pants down his muscular thighs and tossed them aside. Naked, he lay half sprawled before her, a gorgeous powerful male who was all hers.

Quick as she could, Harper shimmied out of her pants and returned to her earlier position on the couch. Without opening his eyes, Ashton ran his hands over the curve of her hips and butt and down the back of her thighs. She gasped when his fingers dipped into the heat of her and stroked deep. Shuddering, she braced her hands against his shoulders and surrendered to the pleasure he gave.

He lifted her so he could fill his mouth with her breast. Harper wrapped her arms around his neck and gave a soft cry as he sucked hard. Pummeled by desire, she rode the waves of pleasure, each one a little stronger than the last.

"Ashton, I can't wait any longer."

He eased her down until she was poised over him. She

was so wet that he slid inside her an inch without meaning to. He intended to savor the anticipation, let the hunger build, but he underestimated Harper's passion. With a smile of sheer bliss she lowered herself onto his shaft, taking him deep. The perfection of her snug fit cradled him in a way that he'd never known before. Almost immediately, she began to move, her hips dancing in a seductive rhythm that slammed into his willpower and sent his lust into overdrive.

Digging his fingers into the soft flesh of her backside, he began to thrust in time with her movements. Her breasts swayed, hypnotically close to his face as she arched her back and surrendered to the pressure building inside her.

A soft keening escaped her parted lips as her skin flushed red. Ashton slowed his movements and deepened each thrust, watching her come apart. Her body bowed, muscles tensing as she climaxed. In this magical place he felt humbled by her vulnerability and her strength. She'd given him her all, held nothing back. She opened her eyes and locked gazes at him.

"That was incredible." She licked her lips and puffed out a breath, then murmured, "Come for me."

At her command, he renewed his drive toward orgasm. He pumped into her, distantly hearing her encouraging words. It was over faster than he would have liked. Her hands on his body, her inner muscles clenching to increase that amazing friction and her teeth on his earlobe sent him spiraling into one hell of a climax. He came for what seemed like forever. The pleasure of his release was almost painful in its intensity.

While the last spasms were fading he wrapped his arms around her slim form and buried his face in her neck. He drifted his fingertips over the bumps of her spine and waited for the hammering in his chest to slow. It hurt to breathe.

"You are amazing," he said.

"You're not so bad yourself." She kissed his neck. "How long do we have until dinner?"

"A couple hours, I think." Sucking in a lungful of her spicy scent, he closed his eyes and imprinted this moment forever on his soul. "But if I don't eat until morning, I'll be fine."

"Won't Franco wonder what happened to us?"

"Oh, he'll know. He got a look at you while you stood beside the pool. And he'll understand if my appetite this evening won't be sated by food."

She poked him in the ribs and made him grunt. "Is there a bathroom in this lovely tent or do we bathe in the river?"

"Only if you wish to meet a crocodile face-to-face." He pushed aside damp strands of her hair and drifted his lips across her cheek, tasting the saltiness of her sweat. "There's an outdoor shower."

"I'm not sure I'm ready for that much adventure."

"Then I won't recommend the fried caterpillars Franco might have on the menu."

Harper shuddered. "I'm sure you'll tell me they're delicious but I'm just going to have to take your word on that."

"There should be a bathroom behind there with a slipper tub." He pointed to the wall behind the wardrobe.

Ashton accepted the perfunctory kiss she dropped onto his lips and watched with appreciation as she padded naked to collect her bag and then head to the bathroom. The last of the afternoon sunlight played over her soft skin, highlighting the different textures of bone, sinew and muscle. She had an athletic body that she pushed hard. In fact, she had it all. Resilient body. Strong mind. Romantic heart. Idealist soul.

Was the last going to survive the meeting with her father? Ashton had a bad feeling about what was to come tomorrow. A man didn't dedicate himself completely to a lifestyle that involved being gone for several months or even a year at a time without understanding it would be difficult to maintain close relationships. A wife and family wouldn't be a top priority.

More than anything Ashton wanted to spare Harper any disappointment Greg LeDay might heap upon her, but she'd come too far to turn back now. The best he could do was be a shoulder to cry on.

Not wishing his solemn mood to put a damper on their evening, Ashton chose to use the shower outside before dressing for dinner. Slipping on a pair of khaki pants and a beige knit shirt, he toyed with his Saint Christopher medal while he waited for Harper to appear. His mother had given the medal to him on a trip back to South Africa. They were traveling by plane. He'd been six. They'd encountered a storm halfway and been tossed around. While lightning darted around the wings, his mother had removed the medal from her neck and fastened it around his, telling him that Saint Christopher, the patron saint of travelers, would protect him.

When he'd left home at fifteen, he'd taken the medal with him and had worn it every day since. Ashton wasn't sure why, whether it was superstition or faith. Whichever it was, it had kept him safe.

He'd spent more time thinking about his parents in the past week than he had in the past twenty years. Being on the front lines of Harper's identity struggle had opened doors he'd thought long locked and barred. What awaited him hadn't been as painful as he'd expected. Having someone he cared about accept him unconditionally had made the difference.

Now all he had to do was offer Harper the same unequivocal support, no matter how misguided he thought her decision to confront her biological father was. He would be there to comfort her if things went awry.

Ten

Harper's fingers bit into the passenger door armrest as the Range Rover neared the camp that Greg LeDay was using as the base for the safari he was leading. The sun was lowering toward the horizon, casting a warm glow over the landscape. This morning they'd overslept and arrived too late to catch LeDay before he took out his clients.

For the past six hours she and Ashton had been driving around Kruger National Park, hoping for a glimpse of wildlife. The roads they'd taken had been paved, and the truck had decent springs, but her stomach wasn't feeling particularly settled. She blamed it on nerves. Soon she would get to meet the man who might be her father.

How it went would determine the rest of her life. There was a great deal riding on the outcome of this meeting.

"Hang in there." Ashton's hand covered hers in a reassuring squeeze. As he'd been doing these past few days, he'd picked up on her mood and knew just what to say.

"I wish I knew how he was going to react."

"Looks like the trucks are back. You should know pretty quick."

Before Ashton threw the Range Rover into Park, she spotted Greg LeDay. He wore khaki-colored cotton pants, a short sleeved beige shirt and a tan vest with six pockets. A wide-brimmed hat in some drab color between gray and brown shielded his face from the sun. But even with that protection, he looked older than the photo on his webpage. Years of living in the bush had etched lines around his eyes and given his skin a look of worn leather.

Heart thumping erratically, Harper approached the group he was addressing. She'd asked Ashton to hang back and give her time to introduce herself. He wasn't happy about her request, but he'd agreed.

LeDay's gaze found her lingering on the fringes of the crowd and dwelled on her for a moment before he returned his attention to his charges. "This was a great day. Tomorrow we'll go out and see if we can't find some cats."

The crowd dispersed, sidestepping Harper, who stood tongue-tied and uncertain. She'd practiced a hundred different openings and none of them seemed right.

"Can I help you?"

"My name is Harper Fontaine." She stumbled over her surname, wondering at the last second if he'd recognize it.

"Nice to meet you." No recognition flared in his eyes.

"I believe you met my mother several years ago. Penelope Fontaine?"

"Was she on one of my safaris?"

Things had just gotten awkward. "You met her in London. At an exhibition of your work."

"I'm sorry. The name just doesn't ring a bell."

"Perhaps a picture would help." Harper pulled out her smartphone and showed him an image of her mother, knowing Penelope would be quite put out that a lover—even one she'd had a brief affair with thirty years prior—could forget her so easily.

LeDay didn't look at the photo; he stared at Harper. "Why don't you tell me what this is about."

"You had an affair with my mother." Now that the words were out, Harper was struck with an awful thought. What if she'd flown halfway around the world to meet the wrong man?

"And if I did?"

"Then I'm your daughter."

Other than a brief tightening of his mouth, LeDay didn't react to her announcement. He regarded Harper in silence for a long time and she started to understand how he'd captured all those incredible moments in his photographs. He had the ability to stay very still for long periods of time. Meanwhile her heart rate was escalating and her breath had gone unsteady.

At last LeDay moved. He crossed his arms over his chest. "What do you want?"

"Nothing." Obviously that wasn't true, but Harper hadn't defined for herself what chasing him halfway around the globe was supposed to accomplish. "I only recently found out. I simply wanted to meet you." Her voice trailed off. His expression hadn't changed. He looked as welcoming as a rock pile.

"Where are you from?"

"I live in Las Vegas at the moment."

"That's a long way to come for nothing."

"I guess I was hoping that getting to know you would help answer some questions I have."

"Are you staying here?"

"No, we drove over from Grant's."

His eyebrows rose. "We?"

Harper turned in Ashton's direction and he left the car and headed toward them. "This is Ashton Croft," she said, catching his hand and drawing him to her side.

The two men shook hands, sizing each other up, like a

pair of competing alpha males. Harper sensed they came to some sort of understanding.

"I've seen your show. You've traveled extensively."

"Experiencing new cultures and cuisine is a passion of mine."

LeDay shifted his attention to Harper, but he continued to speak to Ashton. "It's hard having a career where you're gone all the time and maintaining a relationship."

"I know."

They were two of a kind, Harper realized. Adventure-loving men who didn't want to be tied down. She'd known that going in and didn't want to domesticate Ashton. He'd never be happy staying put for long. He would go wherever the wind blew next. Two questions remained. Would he ever invite her to travel with him? Would she say yes if he did?

LeDay gestured toward the cluster of buildings. "The restaurant has opened for dinner. If you'd like to eat before returning to your camp."

"Would you join us?" Harper asked, barely able to hope he'd agree.

He hesitated and then nodded. Still hand in hand, she and Ashton followed him toward the outdoor dining area. Trembling slightly in reaction to the stress of meeting the man she believed to be her father, Harper leaned her head against Ashton's shoulder.

"You okay?" he asked, his fingers brushing her cheek.

"Just a little overwhelmed."

"That's to be expected."

"I'm glad you're here," she whispered.

He squeezed her hand in response as they followed a waiter to their table. Once they sat down and Harper had a chance to survey the menu, she wasn't sure she'd be able to eat anything. She glanced to Ashton for help.

"Will you order something for me? I can't make up my mind."

"Of course."

The waiter brought beer for the men and a glass of red wine for Harper, wrote down their dinner selections and left.

Harper gathered a breath, surprised by how unsteady she felt, and plunged in. "I know you must be annoyed with me for showing up here like this, and I'm sorry that I didn't give you some warning. But I wasn't sure if you'd see me."

"I'm still not sure I'm the person you're looking for."

"Frankly, neither am I, but my mother said she met a wildlife photographer at an exhibition of his work in London and then she bought a book of your photographs for my grandmother." Hearing herself, Harper broke off. She caught Ashton's gaze and saw reassurance there. "It sounds a bit crazy when I say it out loud."

"Let me see that photo of your mother."

Harper pulled out her phone and handed it to him.

LeDay looked at the photo for a long time before speaking. "Penny."

Penny?

"A beautiful girl."

Harper clapped a hand over her mouth to smother a wild bubble of laughter. It was weird to hear someone call her formal, inflexible mother a girl. Even weirder to hear a man use a nickname in such fond tones. Penelope hated nicknames. And then Harper remembered.

"Her father used to call her that. He died when she was nine."

"We spent almost two weeks together. She was quite the mystery. Had never tasted beer before. Couldn't comprehend how to navigate the Tube. And yet she spoke effortlessly about art, history and politics."

"My mother is fascinated with current events and the background that shaped them. Sometimes I think she knows more about what's going on in Washington, D.C., than the journalists."

"Is she a politician?"

"It's just her hobby."

"What do you do in Las Vegas?"

"My family… I manage a hotel. Fontaine Ciel."

"Fontaine. That's your mother's last name?"

Harper nodded. "Did you know she was married when you were together?"

"She didn't say and wasn't wearing a ring, but I sensed that might have been the case." He paused and stared out over the valley. "What gives you the idea that I'm your father?"

"My father… I recently found out the man I believed was my father was out of town in Macao when I was conceived. My mother isn't the sort of woman to have an affair." Harper glimpsed LeDay's doubt and rushed on. "She was married to a man who cheated on her every chance he got, but I know you were the only time she broke her vows."

"You said you had questions you needed answers to. I don't know what I can tell you."

She hesitated. What had happened to the woman who had all the answers? She never entered a negotiation without a strategy for how to get what she wanted. Beneath the table, Ashton's hand closed over hers, offering support and strength.

"I don't know what to ask. I thought everything would be clear if I met you."

Harper had no choice but to fall silent. Meeting this man hadn't made her confusion disappear. If anything, she was even more lost. As Ashton drew the man out, asking questions about his life in Africa and the magnificent photos he'd taken over the years, Harper listened in fascination and growing dismay. What had she been thinking to come here and expect he would gladly welcome her into his life?

His passion for the country of his birth was all-consuming. The wildlife. The ecosystem. He devoted himself to sharing his experiences and by doing so hoped to increase people's appreciation for the animals and support for his conservation efforts.

A noble cause and one he was ideally suited for. Harper pushed food around on her plate, her appetite nonexistent, and listened with only half her attention until he said something that pulled her out of her thoughts.

"You have two sisters?"

It shocked Harper to think she had aunts she'd never known.

"And a half-dozen nieces and nephews."

"That sounds lovely."

She stopped herself from asking for further details. As much as she longed to hear about this family she'd never known, she remembered what it had been like when her grandfather had told her she had two half sisters. She'd initially viewed them as trespassers in her neatly planned life. This must be how LeDay was feeling. She'd descended into his life without warning and how he must resent her intrusion.

Never mind that Violet and Scarlett had gone from being strangers to family at their first meeting.

"Ashton," she finally said, deciding it was time to stop waiting for some sign that she and LeDay had a connection. The man had enjoyed a brief encounter with a beautiful woman. End of story. That the affair had produced a daughter wasn't going to touch his life. "We should be getting back to camp." She gave LeDay a bright smile. "Thank you for having dinner with us. I enjoyed meeting you."

"Nice meeting you, as well," he replied.

"Ready?" Ashton gave her a searching look.

"Absolutely."

There were no halfhearted offers to stay in touch. Just a simple wave goodbye and a sinking feeling in Harper's stomach that she should have stayed home.

Overwhelmed by futility, Harper trudged back to the car. Her boots felt as if they weighed ten pounds each.

She'd been uncharacteristically naive to expect that she and LeDay would have some sort of immediate connection.

"That didn't go as you'd hoped," Ashton said, stating the obvious. "I suspected he wasn't going to welcome you with open arms."

That he was right didn't make Harper feel any better about how meeting her father had gone. She was angry with herself for wondering if the reason Ross Fontaine hadn't been a loving father was because they weren't biologically related.

"A man like that isn't interested in family," Ashton continued, and Harper wasn't sure if he was trying to make her feel better or just pointing out the obvious. "He has his photography and the safaris. They're his passion. He doesn't seem to need anyone."

Weighed down by disappointment, Harper's temper got the better of her. "Like someone else I know?"

"Criticize me all you want, but I'm here for you."

As she threw herself into the Range Rover and waited for him to get behind the wheel, she wondered what he did feel about her. The way he'd made love to her left her emotions jumbled and her confidence rocky. Could a man kiss with such gut-wrenching passion and feel nothing more than uncomplicated lust? Ashton wasn't exactly the easiest person to read and she couldn't expect him to start spouting poetry.

Who was Ashton Croft? Selfish adventurer? Celebrity hound? Romantic lover?

Seeing that Ashton continued to stand where she'd left him, Harper got out of the vehicle and crossed to stand before him. Hands bracketing his hips, he was staring at the distant horizon, a scowl of absolute frustration drawing his brows together. If he'd noticed she'd reappeared, he gave no sign.

"How do I make you feel?" she asked softly, scarcely

able to believe she had the nerve to have her heart stomped all over for a second time that day.

"Dependable." He made the word sound like a curse.

It wasn't at all what she expected him to say, and the giddy relief that struck her made little sense. "You don't like being dependable?"

"I don't like living up to anyone's expectations but my own."

"I wish you could teach me your trick of living that way."

He cupped her face in his hands and kissed her hard. She met the bold thrust of his tongue with matching hunger and let herself be swept up in the rising passion of their embrace. This was easy. Surrendering to his mastery. Letting his insistent kisses and eager hands sweep away all her worries.

Breathing unevenly, Ashton placed his forehead against hers. They stayed that way for several minutes as the sun sank below the horizon and the night sounds swelled. At long last he stirred.

"We'd better get going. It's an hour back to camp."

She nodded and let him draw her back to the truck. As the ancient shocks struggled to absorb the road's dips and bumps, Harper reflected over the past few hours.

"You know it doesn't matter that LeDay disappointed me," she said, determination in her voice. "In fact, I'm glad. I can stop second-guessing who I am. I can go back to my life and my career and never look back again. It's better for everyone this way."

Ashton's features could have been carved from stone. "You're not going to tell your grandfather the truth about who your father really is."

"Why should I?"

"Because maybe if you know you'll never be Fontaine's CEO you might look around and see there's something you'd rather be doing."

"Being CEO is what I want."

"Then why did you hop on a plane at the last second and fly all this way to meet your father? You could have saved time and money by staying home and making the same decision."

He was right. "I became a businesswoman because that's what my father and grandfather did. It defined me. Then I find out I'm not a businessman's daughter, but the offspring of a brilliant photographer. I know I should take something away from that, but I don't know what."

"Who your parents are doesn't define you any more than your environment does. You are the sum of your choices."

"You're a fool to believe your parents didn't define you. You've spent your whole life rejecting their selflessness and believing you're out for no one but yourself."

"At least I admit that I'm selfish. It's my parents who are hypocrites. They were so obsessed with their mission to save every person they met that they couldn't take two minutes to recognize the person closest to them needed their help, as well."

Ashton made the accusation without heat or bitterness, as if he'd made peace with his parents' flaws long ago. By proclaiming his own selfishness he warned the world what they could expect from him.

Harper's heart constricted in sympathy.

"So you ran away and got caught up with a bad group."

"I was fifteen and my parents never tried to find me." And there was the crux of all his pain. Abandoned. Left to fend for himself. Terrorized for three years. Of course he'd developed a protective shell.

"How do you know that? The criminals you fell in with needed to stay way below the radar. They couldn't have been easy for the police to find."

"My parents never filed a report that I was missing. No one was looking for me." He took one hand off the wheel and pinched the bridge of his nose. "When I first joined the gang, Franco checked. Couldn't find anyone looking for a fifteen-year-old white kid. He told me to go home, offered to help me get out."

"Why didn't you?"

"Go home to what? I'd left because my parents didn't give a damn about me. Nothing had changed. They went on with their work. That's what was important to them."

The unfairness of it burned like acid in Harper's stomach. She knew loneliness. Hadn't she been an afterthought in her parents' lives? Ross Fontaine had taken to fatherhood with less enthusiasm than he'd put into being a husband. But her situation hadn't been unique among her classmates. Many of them had successful, driven parents who worked eighty hours a week and traveled extensively.

But she couldn't imagine any of them losing a child and going on as if nothing had happened.

"Do you ever wonder what happened to them?"

For a moment Ashton regretted sharing his past with Harper. She wasn't good at leaving things alone. That her journey to self-discovery hadn't ended well wasn't going to diminish her confidence for long. He was certain by the time they got on the plane tomorrow that she would have the plan for her future all documented with bullet points and colorful graphs.

"I don't wonder." Or he hadn't until she'd raised the question. Franco had offered to track down his parents on several occasions, but Ashton had turned him down each time. If they hadn't looked for him, why should he make sure they were doing all right? "They were committed to their ministry. Whatever happened to them, they will not regret the sacrifices they made."

And for that he couldn't condemn them. They'd chosen a path that gave them satisfaction. He'd done the same. He accepted that they wouldn't be proud that he'd made a great deal of money and become famous. Nothing about what he did fell into their value system.

"I envy your ability to put your past behind you like that."

He wasn't completely sure he'd attained the sort of peace of mind she believed he had. Returning to Africa had raised too many old ghosts. He might have left his life here behind fifteen years ago, but it had shaped him into the man he was. That wasn't something he could completely escape.

They were silent for the rest of the drive back to the camp, the barrier between them created by his stubbornness and her disappointment. Ashton was aware of a sharp ache in his chest. It was a sensation he hadn't felt in a long time. Harper's questions about his parents had unlocked the door on regret. Wanting to know if his mother and father were all right meant he cared. By caring about them he betrayed himself, and the choice he'd made to put his needs first because they never had.

Being selfish at thirty-five wasn't the same as acting out when he was fifteen. In the years since he'd left home, he'd learned to feel compassion for others the way his parents hoped he would. Even if he hated to admit it and seemed to live his life as if it wasn't the case, they'd had a powerful influence on him. Maybe it was past time he surrendered to it.

The walkways and outdoor areas of the tent camp were lit with softly glowing oil lamps by the time the Range Rover rolled into a parking space. Ashton glanced at Harper and saw her gaze was fixed on the fanciful beauty of the camp nestled among thousands of acres of wild African countryside.

He took her hand as they traversed the raised walkway to their tent. Although she neither looked his way, nor offered any inkling of her thoughts, she spread her fingers and welcomed the connection.

To Ashton's great surprise, she began stripping out of her clothes as soon as they entered the tent. Given her difficult day, he expected her to want distance and space. But as she came to stand naked before him and attacked his buttons with single-minded intensity, he decided not to question her motivation.

They tumbled into the big soft bed in a tangle of tongues and limbs. Ashton made love to her with demanding passion, offering no tenderness. She seemed to need none. Her movements beneath him were feverish. Fingernails bit into his skin. Teeth found sensitive areas and left marks.

At last he settled between her thighs, spreading them wide so she would feel a tiny spark of helplessness. Her head thrashed on the pillow as his size and weight pinned her to the mattress, but he hesitated before joining their bodies. He wanted her to recognize his strength, wanted to demonstrate what it felt like to be at his mercy. His power, his determination would protect her from anything, but she had to let him.

As she reached out to touch him, he grasped her wrists and pinned them above her head. She fought his hold, glaring at him the whole time. It wasn't until her lashes fell and her muscles relaxed that he shifted his hips forward and slid his entire length into her.

Almost immediately her body began to shake with release. He pushed deeper, and she began to cry out. He released her wrists and meshed their fingers, withdrawing so he could drive into her a second time. The strength and swiftness of her climax stirred an uproar in his own body and he followed her over the edge in a matter of seconds.

They lay panting in the aftermath. Ashton shifted to lie on his back and drew her snugly against his side. She fit against him with such blissful perfection that he closed his eyes to savor the moment. For a long time the only sound in the room was their breathing and the muted tick of the clock on the nightstand. Before long, however, as their bodies settled into normal rhythms, he realized the buzzing in his ears wasn't the pounding of his blood through his veins, but the nighttime chorus of cicadas and frogs.

"Hear that?" Ashton whispered.

Beside him, Harper held her breath and listened. From far off came the sound of someone trying to get a chainsaw going with short quick pulls of the start cord. "Yes."

"That's a leopard call."

A thrill of excitement raced down her arms. "It sounds close."

"Probably a half mile away."

Safe in Ashton's embrace, she snuggled her face into the crook of his neck and smiled. No one could be in better hands than her right now. Absently she traced the scar crisscrossing his abdomen. When she'd touched it before, he'd seemed to withdraw from her. Despite her curiosity, she hadn't asked him to expand on his days with the gang. This time, he might be more open to her inquisitiveness.

"More knife play?"

His answer took a long time coming. "Yes."

Hearing the tightness in his voice, she held silent. They were old scars. From a lifetime ago. Long healed, but permanent reminders of what…?

Beneath her hand his torso rose and fell on a deep breath. The force of it ruffled the hair scattered across her shoulder and tickled her skin.

"Chapman didn't hire weaklings." His voice sounded ghostly in the dim room. "Everyone had to prove they could fight. Even a fifteen-year-old boy whose only knife experience had come from slicing vegetables." His short laugh held no amusement. "He was a sadistic bastard. Once a week he pitted one of his crew against another in sporting matches. Some sport. Whoever drew first blood won. Three losses and you were out." Ashton threw his forearm over his eyes. "Throat slit, dumped in the jungle for the scavengers to feast on."

Harper couldn't imagine what this had been like for a teenager. "Why'd anyone stay working for him?"

"He made them rich. How do you think Franco could open this place?"

"Why did you stay?"

"I was proving a point to my parents."

"At the risk of your life?"

"Who doesn't think they're invincible at fifteen? I was big for my age. I'd gotten into a lot of trouble fighting the neighborhood kids. What I lacked was the technique to fight with a knife. Franco took me under his wing right away, but I didn't learn fast enough and lost two weeks in a row."

"So Chapman wanted you dead?"

Ashton shook his head. "I don't think so. The pairings were random. It was bad luck is all. My second bout I almost took the guy out. His reach was longer, but he was bulky and I was fast." He caught her fingers and drew them to a spot on his left side just below the ribs. "A wild swing caught me here. It took twenty stitches to sew me up."

"You're lucky you didn't die from infection."

"My luck turned when Chapman didn't pull my name for two months. I spent a lot of time with Franco after that. Never lost again."

The strain in Ashton's voice betrayed the toll that had taken on him. He might not have killed anyone directly, but he had to know that by saving himself he was signing someone else's death warrant. From missionaries' son to criminal to world-renowned chef.

"You can't forgive yourself."

"Should I?"

"What happened wasn't your fault. Chapman's game went on whether you were there or not. Those men made a choice just as you did. And you got out."

"But I never turned him in. When the opportunity presented itself I ran."

And pursued by guilt he'd been running ever since.

"Do you really want the cooking show in New York?"

she asked. "I can't help but feel you'll be turning your back on what made you successful."

"And what is that?"

"You thrived in situations that would terrify most people. Every episode contained an edge of danger that kept me glued to the TV."

"As much as I enjoyed doing the show, I'm looking to change my image. Go more mainstream." He rolled away from her and sat with his legs hanging off the side of the bed, his back toward her. "The network is going to push it hard. My popularity will skyrocket. It's what I've been working for."

"And all this time I thought it was the joy of food that motivated you." If he hoped to find legitimacy in success, how high did his star have to rise before he could be at peace with what he'd done to survive?

"More viewers means my culinary point of view reaches more people."

With their earlier rapport slipping away, Harper left the bed and slipped into a pair of leggings and a sweater. She handed Ashton his clothes and waited in silence while he put them on. Then she drew him out onto the deck and stood beside him near the rail, looking out over the river.

Surrounded by the night sounds it was easy to feel one with the bush. For several minutes they listened without speaking. One call was repeated several times, causing Harper to break the quiet.

"What is that?"

"A baboon sounding an alarm. Probably because of the leopard we heard earlier."

"You were right when you said we're the sum of our experiences. The things that you've been through had a profound effect on the man you've become. If you'd stayed with your parents you wouldn't resent them any less, but your strength of will might never have been tested and you might never have discovered the heights of your courage."

Harper paused to let her words sink in. "But I'm right, too. You inherited their generosity of spirit and desire to help those less fortunate. How many thousands of people have been helped through the foundations you promote?"

"I'm nothing more than a spokesman. I don't tangibly help anyone."

"What about Dae? You saved him from going to prison for something he didn't do and taught him how to cook. Someday he'll run one of your restaurants. How far is that from where he started?"

Ashton bumped his shoulder against her, forcing her to step to the side in order to maintain her balance. His fingers snaked around her waist and pulled her against his side. "This was supposed to be your journey to self-discovery, not mine."

"Ironic, isn't it?" Suddenly she felt a weight lift off her shoulders. "You know what? I don't care about the man who impregnated my mother. He doesn't want to be anyone's father. Why should I take that personally and cry about it?" She gripped the railing hard. "I need to worry about me."

"So, you've decided what to do when you get home?"

"I'm going to do what everyone expects of me and keep my mother's secret. I came to South Africa in search of who I am. Now I know. I'm Harper Fontaine. Future CEO of Fontaine Hotels and Resorts. I've worked my whole life to run the company. I don't know who else to be."

"And that's all you need to make you happy in the long run?"

"It's been my goal since I was five, so, achieving it will bring me great satisfaction."

"I hope you're right."

Eleven

Harper woke to an empty bed and a heavy heart. From the light outside she gathered it was a few hours after sunrise. She sat up and glanced around the tent, but from the room's low energy level, she could tell Ashton wasn't nearby. Flopping back onto the pillows, she closed her eyes and willed herself to stop feeling so vulnerable and out of sorts. It wasn't as if she hadn't endured setbacks in her life before. Failure was a necessary part of growing. But one emotional blow after the other had weakened her ability to recover swiftly.

Still, she did recover and an hour after waking, she was showered, dressed, packed and on her way to breakfast. That Ashton still hadn't made an appearance didn't bother her. He and Franco hadn't spent much time together since they'd arrived. Ashton was probably with his old friend. Or maybe taking a walk along the river. There were several trails around the camp.

Harper was accustomed to spending a great deal of time

alone. Being surrounded by staff wasn't like sharing a bathroom and a bed with someone. The intimacy she'd enjoyed with Ashton these past few days had been pretty all-consuming. She wouldn't blame him if he needed a break.

And she needed to get used to being without him. She had no illusions about their relationship. It was an interlude, similar to what her mother had enjoyed with LeDay. A break from routine. A wonderful adventure. Harper recognized that she couldn't hold on to Ashton. His career took him all over the world. Hers kept her grounded in one place.

Except he was on the verge of doing a show that would keep him in New York for an extended period of time. They could be together if she accepted the job of Fontaine's CEO. Unfortunately, he'd made her question if that was the best choice for her.

As she was finishing up her breakfast, Ashton found her. She didn't ask him where he'd been and he didn't volunteer the information. His mouth was set in a grim line as he sat down across from her and poured himself a cup of coffee from the silver pot on the table.

"Are you okay?" she asked, unable to shake the feeling that their magical trip was over.

"Fine."

"Have you eaten?"

"I had a little something earlier." He sipped his coffee and stared past her. "I saw that you're packed."

"I wasn't sure what time the plane would be returning us to Johannesburg so I thought I'd be ready to leave."

"I told them noon."

Harper checked her watch. If they left in the next fifteen minutes, they would be right on time. She reached out her hand and placed it over his, calling his attention back to her.

"Thank you for coming to Africa to help me. I've really appreciated having you here."

"No need to thank me."

His short replies were starting to irritate her. She needed

to get to the bottom of it before they started the long journey home.

"So this is it then?"

"What do you mean?"

"The end of the road for us. It was a fun week, but now it's over."

"Is that what you want?"

"No." Her throat tightened, but she'd taken too many emotional risks to let fear dominate her now. "I want for us to be together." For the first time she understood Violet's decision to put her marriage before her ambition. "It would be nice to hear that you feel the same."

"Are you sure you really know what you want? A few days ago you couldn't wait to run off to Africa to meet your biological father. What would you have done if he'd wanted to have a relationship with you? Would you have stayed in Africa? Made a new life here?"

"I don't know. I hadn't thought that far ahead."

"Then last night you decided you weren't going to let anything stand in the way of your becoming CEO. You claim you want to know who you are, yet instead of pushing forward and doing what you want for a change, you fall back into old patterns."

Was Ashton asking her to quit the hotel business and spend the rest of her life…doing what?

She still didn't know her true passion. Damn him for being right. And for being the practical one for a change. She needed the old Ashton, the impulsive one, to sweep her into adventure. She was sick of planning her future. She'd come to Africa because she wanted to be bold and daring. But obviously that wasn't her nature. It had taken less than a week before she regressed to comfortable patterns. What she needed to do was take a risk and keep taking them until she felt completely free.

"I love you," she said, captured by a yearning that grew

stronger the more time she spent with Ashton. "I can't imagine my days without you. I'm ready to give up everything and be with you. Just tell me you want me."

Ashton closed his eyes. "I don't want you to give up anything."

"Then what do you want?"

"Don't use me as an excuse to avoid admitting who you are and what you truly want."

"I already told you, I want you."

"Because it's easier to explain to your grandfather that you want to be with the man you love than disappoint him by revealing you're not actually his granddaughter?"

"That's unfair."

"Is it?"

She couldn't answer him truthfully so she traded him question for question. "What about you?"

"What about me?"

"Would you give up the new show and go back to doing *The Culinary Wanderer* again?" It wasn't fair to ask him to set aside his goals. So what if she didn't think he would be happy. They'd been lovers for little more than a week. Who was she to judge what was best for him?

"I already quit and I don't want to go backward."

Her heart sank. "Then you're going to do whatever it takes to make the new network want you."

"That's the plan."

"Then I guess we're destined to disappoint each other, aren't we?"

"I don't believe that's true."

Was his faith so much greater than hers? She wished she could do as he asked and start over, but she'd tried that when she'd come here to meet her father and look how poorly that had turned out.

Her phone chimed. A text message from Violet had come in.

Grandfather has had a mild stroke. He's going to be okay. Wants to see you.

A sound in her ears swelled as if every insect in the entire bush had chosen that moment to sing. Disoriented, she shook her head to clear it. Ashton grabbed her hand and said something that she couldn't catch, but she guessed he was asking her what was wrong.

With her voice unable to escape her tight throat, she showed him the message.

"You should call and let them know we're coming."

"We?" she whispered. "You're coming with me?"

"Whatever you need from me. I'll be there."

Ashton didn't expect to be heading to Las Vegas mere hours after completing the transatlantic flight from Johannesburg. While the charter jet he'd hired cruised over the heartland of the U.S., he fidgeted with his phone, restlessly checking for updated emails and new texts, knowing if anything came in he would be notified with a tone.

That he'd left Harper behind wasn't sitting well, but she'd insisted. An hour before they'd touched down at JFK, she'd sat straighter in her seat and gathered herself. He'd gotten used to taking care of her these past few days. Discovered he liked that she needed him. But with their return to the States, her independent nature had reasserted itself.

And she'd been right when she'd insisted the restaurant was days away from opening. He needed to be at Batouri overseeing the last-minute details. He should have been there these past five days instead of traveling to South Africa. But Dae's updates had reassured him that the staff was working well together. Chef Cole had proven to be a good choice. He was organized and a good leader. Harper had been right about that.

When his phone chimed, it wasn't the person he'd been hoping to hear from. Vince had sent him a terse text.

Call me.

The brevity of the message could only mean the network had decided to take the cooking show in a different direction and not use him. Ashton had been expecting this ever since he'd walked out and was surprised how little he cared. In the past few days he'd had a lot of time to think. Conversations with Harper regarding her ambivalence toward her career left him debating what he wanted to do versus what he thought he should do.

"Vince," he said as soon as his manager picked up. "What's the word?"

"Lifestyle Network wants you."

Ashton didn't feel the rush of satisfaction he'd expected. "That's not the impression I got from the last meeting."

"They took another look at the tape and saw what I see. You're a star. Soon every household in America is going to know it. They sent me a contract. I've looked it over and everything we asked for is in there."

"I need a few days to think about it."

Silence greeted his response. Ashton imagined his manager was pretty pissed at him right now.

"I've put in a lot of time on this deal," Vince said. "They're giving us everything we want except for the whole *Culinary Wanderer* thing, but you've already quit, so that's a nonfactor."

"Frankly, Vince, when I left the conference room last Monday I was under the impression they wanted to go a different way."

"But they don't."

With nothing standing in the way of signing onto the new show, Ashton had to tackle the doubts raised by his conversation with Harper. "I'm questioning whether staying put in New York is the best thing for me."

Vince's disappointment came through the phone seconds before he spoke. "I wish I'd known that three days ago."

"Why don't we table this for a while. I need to focus on the restaurant right now. Send me the contract and give me a few days to sort through everything."

"Sending it now. Don't leave them hanging too long about this."

"I won't."

When he received Vince's email a minute later, Ashton scanned through the contract with only half his mind on the words. He could really use Harper's input on this. But the last thing he wanted to do right now was disturb her. She had enough on her plate.

Maybe he could talk to her when she returned to Las Vegas for the opening. If she returned. It occurred to him with her grandfather out of commission, it was a perfect time for her to step into the role she'd been training for. She'd decided to follow her head not her heart. He wasn't convinced that was the right decision. And now he had the project that would allow him to be with her. If only it all felt right.

Harper entered her grandfather's New York apartment and was immediately embraced by Violet. The warmth of her greeting was a delightful contrast to the indifference Harper had felt from LeDay. Biology didn't make a family. Caring did.

"How's grandfather?"

"Much better," Violet said, reaching her hand back to her husband for support. JT Stone put his arm around his wife and hugged gently. "He's already protesting the doctor's order to rest."

"Did the stroke cause any permanent damage?"

"From what Dr. Amhull told us, it was a very minor stroke so there shouldn't be any lasting effects. It was a warning that worse could come. He prescribed medication and wants Grandfather to slow down."

"Can I go see him?"

"Of course. And afterward, I think we should talk. Scarlett and Logan went for a walk. They should be back shortly. The six of us should sit down before dinner. There are some things we think you should know."

"The six of us?"

"Isn't Ashton in New York with you?"

"The restaurant is opening in a few days." Harper's stomach turned over as she pictured his tight expression when she told him to go on to Las Vegas without her. "He needs to be in Vegas for that."

Violet stared at her a long moment before nodding. "Of course."

Further explanations would have to wait until later. The most important thing was seeing her grandfather. "Is Grandfather in his room?"

"No. He's in his study. We confiscated his cell phone to keep him from working, but nothing can convince him to stay in bed."

Harper shook her head as she walked down the hallway toward her grandfather's favorite room in the apartment. His work ethic had inspired her own. They were so much alike. Maybe that's why it had been such a shock to discover they weren't related.

She found him sitting in one of a pair of leather chairs that flanked the fireplace. He had a stack of magazines on the table beside him eight inches high. Pausing in the doorway, she scrutinized him. His color was better than she'd expected, and he was scowling at the article he was perusing. Temper was a positive sign.

"Grandfather?"

He looked up from his reading and waved her over. "This is nothing but a fluff piece." The page he showed her had a photo of Gil Kurtz, one of her grandfather's classmates from Harvard and a Connecticut state senator. They'd been rivals since they were twenty years old, and

Henry rarely had anything but disparaging things to say about Gil's political career.

"How are you feeling?"

"I'm fine. Your sisters won't let me leave the house. Don't they understand I have a business to run?"

"They're just concerned about you."

"Violet said you were in Africa. Feel like telling me what you were doing there?"

"I just needed a little break."

Her grandfather grunted. "Bob tried not to give me the impression you'd cracked up, but wasn't able to mask his concern."

"Cracked up?" She laughed a little at the thought. "Why?"

"Because you dropped the entire running of the hotel on him and disappeared."

"I took a vacation."

"When was the last time you took any substantial time off?"

"I don't know." She thought back over the past few years and couldn't recall a span of more than three days where she'd been unavailable to her staff. "Which should make it even more evident I needed a vacation."

"The last time was when I told you about Scarlett and Violet."

"Was it?" She had a vague recollection of going to her grandmother's Hamptons house for a few days.

"You were gone almost two weeks."

"Sorry, but I don't recall that. And I'm sure I had the time coming."

"You did. And much more besides. You're more like me than your father." He was staring out the window at the park across the street. "But occasionally you remind me that you're also your mother's daughter. She's an emotional woman who has difficulty handling any sort of turmoil in her life. Which leads me to wonder what is going on with you. Is that Croft fellow causing problems?"

"Ashton?" Harper was more than a little stunned by her grandfather's analysis of her. He never appeared to notice anything that didn't pertain to his business, but now she wondered if he saw everything and just kept it to himself. "No, he and I have reached a place where we're working well together."

"How about your personal relationship? Everything okay there, too?"

"Ah…" What was he asking? "We work well together."

Her grandfather blew out an impatient breath. "I'm not dense. I know you went to Africa with him."

"Technically, I went to Africa and he followed."

"Why?"

What was her grandfather asking? "Why did he follow me to Africa?"

"Yes. And why did you go in the first place?"

"I wanted an adventure, and Ashton thought I was acting recklessly by traveling alone. Turns out he was a little right."

"More than a little. You were mugged on the train. Had your passport stolen."

How was she going to keep the truth about her biological father hidden when her grandfather was so good at keeping tabs on her?

"Who told you?"

"When I heard you were traveling to South Africa I called a buddy of mine in the State Department and had him keep an eye out for you."

Harper was both touched and annoyed. Didn't anyone think she could take care of herself? "Is that why I was able to get a temporary passport so fast?"

"Partially." Her grandfather's eyes narrowed. "Anything else you'd like to tell me about your time in South Africa?"

"Ashton took me on safari where I was fortunate enough

to see three of the big five. Elephants, cape buffalo and lions." She paused. "Although one night we heard a leopard, as well."

"And that's all?"

"It's a beautiful country. We should consider putting a hotel there."

"Maybe when you become CEO of Fontaine Hotels and Resorts you can do that."

The walls of her grandfather's study seemed to close in. Ashton's warning sounded in her mind. She wanted to silence it, but couldn't. He was right. Becoming CEO under false pretenses would never make her happy. "When that happens, I'll definitely look into it."

They chatted about her impression of Africa until Scarlett appeared in the doorway.

"Can I tear you away for a bit?" she asked Harper, giving Henry a fond smile.

"Sure."

"Are you staying for dinner?" he asked. Despite his protests that he was feeling fine, he looked pale.

"Of course," Harper said. She kissed his cheek and followed Scarlett from the room.

"He looks better than I expected."

Scarlett linked her arm through Harper's and guided her toward the den. "You probably thought he'd be in bed."

"I did."

Inside the comfortable room, Violet, JT and Logan awaited her. Feeling very much like a fifth wheel, Harper sat down in a chair and waited until everyone else had been seated before she broke the silence.

"You all look so grim. What's going on?"

"How did your trip to South Africa turn out?" Violet began.

Sensing they were warming up to the difficult topic, Harper decided to play along. "It's a lovely country. I told Grandfather we should look at putting a hotel there."

"And what did he think of that?" Again Violet.

Scarlett rolled her eyes. "Stop dancing around what we want to know." Her tone was exasperated. "Did you meet your father?"

"Yes."

"How did it go?"

"No worse than you'd imagine. Being confronted by a twenty-nine-year-old daughter he never knew caught him by surprise."

"Was he courteous?" Violet asked.

"He invited Ashton and me to dinner."

Scarlet piped up. "Where is Ashton?"

"On his way to Las Vegas. The restaurant is opening in two days. I have no idea if it will go well."

"I'm sure it will be fine," Violet said. She glanced at Scarlett and then at JT, who nodded. "Logan was able to figure out who blackmailed your mother."

In the craziness of the past week, Harper had forgotten that little tidbit. "Who?"

JT spoke. "My father. He needed money for a top-notch defense lawyer."

"How did he come by the files?"

"It's my fault," Scarlett said. "If I hadn't brought them home, I wouldn't have lost them."

"You didn't lose them," Logan reminded her, a muscle popping in his jaw. "Someone broke into your suite, knocked you out and stole them."

"Technically," she countered, "I opened the door thinking it was you."

Violet stepped in. "I blame Tiberius. If he hadn't poked his nose in where it didn't belong there wouldn't have been any files in the first place."

"It was my father who went after the information my uncle had gathered on him and hired the guy who hurt Scarlett. He's the one who blackmailed Harper's mother," JT chimed in.

Harper shut her eyes and let the voices wash over her. She floated in darkness until someone touched her arm and brought her back.

Logan knelt before her, his dark brown gaze confident and reassuring. "We retrieved both the information and the money."

She sandwiched Logan's hand between hers, leaned forward and kissed him on the cheek. "Thank you."

"No need to thank me."

She gazed from him to her sisters and finally to JT. This was her family, she realized. Not some stranger in South Africa who wanted nothing to do with her.

"I'm so lucky to have all of you," she told them.

"So, now that your secret is safe," Violet began, "are you going to take the CEO job?"

This was important to all of them, she realized. It meant that Scarlett could continue pursuing her acting and Violet could stay in Las Vegas with JT. They expected her to do the job she was trained for.

"Whenever grandfather wants me to take over, I will."

Twelve

Two hours before the restaurant opened for the first time, Batouri's kitchen was operating more smoothly than Ashton had a right to expect. After being gone during the week before their grand opening, he'd half feared he was coming back to absolute chaos. Thanks to Cole, this was not the case.

Without any major crisis to deal with, Ashton had too much space to think. He tried to focus on the food, but bits of conversations with Harper kept intruding. He second-guessed how he'd handled things when she'd told him she loved him. Had it been a mistake to question her sudden change of heart? He'd been on the verge of sweeping her into his arms and agreeing to make all her dreams come true when the message about her grandfather's stroke had come to her phone.

Carlo approached him. "Harper is here. She's asking for you."

Ashton followed Carlo from the kitchen, struggling to

keep from rushing past the restaurant manager in his excitement to see Harper. She stood by the hostess stand, tense and uncertain in a white dress that draped her slim form in wispy layers of lace. Her hair had been pulled back from her face and loosely clipped in a romantic style. The impact of her appearance stole his breath.

He crossed to her and gave her a kiss on the cheek. From her surprised expression, she'd obviously expected something different.

"I haven't heard from you," he said, making no attempt to hide his unhappiness. "How is your grandfather?"

"The stroke was minor and he's stubborn. Keeping him at home for the past few days has been a challenge when he already feels strong enough to go back to work."

"I'm glad to hear it. What did you tell him about South Africa?"

"That it's a lovely country."

Her answer disappointed him. "That's not what I meant. Did you tell your grandfather the truth about LeDay and your mother?"

"He's just had a stroke. It would be cruel of me to burden him with such a shock." She looked down at her hands. "And thanks to Logan, my mother's blackmailer has been stopped."

"You don't ever plan to tell him." He saw the truth in the way she was avoiding meeting his gaze. "You don't think he'll love you anymore if you're not his flesh and blood."

"Five years ago he went looking for Violet and Scarlett simply because they were his granddaughters. He loves them. What's to say he wouldn't stop loving me when he finds out we're not related?"

"You don't really believe he would do that."

"I don't." Her voice didn't rise above a whisper. "But I can't take the chance. And they're all counting on me."

"Who?"

"My sisters. JT and Logan. They're happy. Their lives

are perfect exactly as they are. If I don't take over as CEO either Scarlett or Violet will have to and neither one wants the job."

In a flash, he saw the future unfold. She would take the CEO job and live in New York City. He would move on to bigger and better things with the new show. The network was ready to get behind him and push him into superstar range. There would be more shows, more opportunities to expand his career. Most important, he and Harper could start a life together.

But was it the life either of them wanted?

"Can we talk about this later?" he asked.

"There's no need. I think you've told me everything you need to."

"Not by a long shot." But he could tell she wasn't listening. "Meet me after the restaurant closes tonight."

"I have too much hotel business to take care of before I fly back to New York tomorrow afternoon. I promised Grandfather that I would step into his shoes for a while. It was the only way I could get him to rest and not worry about the company."

"When will you be back?"

She shook her head. "I'm not sure. It might be a permanent move."

Ashton's heart sank. She would spend the rest of her life living a lie. He wanted what was best for her and this wasn't it. But there was a bright spot to her decision.

"Then I guess we'll be seeing a lot of each other. Lifestyle Network agreed to most of my demands."

"Not all?" Her half-smile was wry.

Ashton gave a one-shoulder shrug. "Those I didn't get aren't all that important."

"You're going to do the show?"

"It means we can be together in New York."

She avoided his gaze. "You know you'll hate being stuck in the city."

"I don't know that." Her lack of enthusiasm for their upcoming proximity left him questioning whether she wanted him in her life. "New York has a lot to offer in terms of culinary experiences."

"Did you agree to cut your hair?"

"It's part of the rebranding."

"Don't do it." She reached up and swept her fingers into his hair, tugging his head down. "Promise me."

"I can't. They're right. In order to appeal to a wider audience, I need a different look."

"You won't look like you."

"It's just hair."

"It's not. It's part of your image. You are the daring adventurer. The guy that charges into dangerous locales and bravely eats whatever exotic fare the population considers typical."

"I can't be that guy the rest of my life."

"Why not?" She stared at him intently. "That's the man I fell in love with."

Her words hit him square in the breastbone. Living without her these past few days had been hell. He couldn't face a future apart from her. But telling her that he loved her wasn't going to make the problem between them go away.

"Because I realized after meeting your father that the traveling I do keeps me apart from people I care about. I don't want to be alone the rest of my life. I want you."

"You can have me and all the adventures you could ever want."

"A part-time relationship with you isn't what I had in mind."

Then her lips were on his and his arms went around her slim body. The kiss was frantic and tasted like goodbye. Ashton's heart was a bowling ball in his chest by the time her lips peeled away from his.

"We're good together," she said.

"The key word is *together*." He cupped her face and

kissed her lightly on the lips. "Tell your grandfather the truth and we can go adventuring together."

"I thought you wanted the Lifestyle Network show."

"I'd rather have you happy and whole."

"Then you understand how I feel about you." She grabbed his hands and pulled them away from her face. "Do the show. It's what's right for your career."

"In the past few weeks I've decided I'm more than my career. What about you?"

She wouldn't meet his gaze. "It's getting late. Shouldn't you be in the kitchen inspiring your staff?"

Ashton eyed her set expression and wondered what would change her mind about permanently taking over as Fontaine's CEO. With a tight nod, he gently kissed her forehead.

"I'll see you in the restaurant later."

"Good luck tonight." With those parting words, she was gone.

With the opening of Batouri mere hours away, Ashton should have been completely consumed by what was happening in his kitchen. He wasn't. Reporters and food critics as well as celebrities and other assorted VIPs would be among the evening's guests. They were expecting a masterful culinary performance tonight. He needed to score big.

That would be easier if Harper hadn't shown up in his kitchen this afternoon. Telling himself that keeping her feet to the fire was for her own good didn't unravel the knot of misery in his chest.

It wasn't until service was well underway that he had a chance to step out of the kitchen and circulate through the room. Before he'd ever stepped in front of a camera, he'd been a successful executive chef and restaurant owner. He recognized a satisfied crowd when he saw one.

As he schmoozed those who could make or break Batouri with a single negative review, he tried not to make it obvious that there was only one table in the room that held his complete attention. And it was the last one he visited.

"Absolutely fabulous," Scarlett said, the first to speak up. The vivacious, stunningly beautiful brunette glanced away from Ashton and nudged Harper's arm. "My sister's idea to have you open a restaurant in her hotel was nothing short of brilliant."

"Wonderful," Violet agreed, a note of concern beneath her upbeat tone. "I think you two make a terrific team."

"That's nice of you to say, but I'm sure your sister would disagree." Ashton had no idea why he felt like baiting Harper on a night where he needed her complete support. Maybe it was the fact that she was looking through him rather than at him. "In fact, the success of the restaurant should be placed squarely at her feet. She smoothed every feather I ruffled in the construction process and probably had to stop the chefs I interviewed from adding arsenic to the food they served me."

Scarlett laughed in delight.

Violet looked appalled.

Harper glared at him. "It's your food everyone loves."

"You were the one who inspired me." The room fell away as he captured her gaze and held it. For a second he saw past her unhappiness and glimpsed the passion she'd demonstrated in Africa. His heart stopped. Maybe there was hope for them yet. He shifted his attention to her sisters and offered them a smile. "Thank you for coming to support Harper."

Not waiting for a response, he moved off.

Behind him, Scarlett spoke up. "Do whatever you have to, but don't let that man get away."

Harper said something in reply, but it was too faint for him to catch. Still, he was feeling better than he had in days as he reentered the kitchen. Nothing was a done deal. Persuading her to be true to herself would be a lot easier if he showed her how to do it.

* * *

At a little after six in the afternoon the day after Batouri's successful opening, Harper entered her grandfather's apartment and found him in the living room, his cell phone in one hand, a glass of Scotch in the other. This is how she imagined he'd go out: running his business while relaxing at home. Working was as much a part of him as breathing. Is this what she wanted for her own life?

Spotting her, he gestured her in. "Sam, I have to go. My granddaughter just arrived, and we're going to have dinner together."

As soon as he hung up, she came forward and hugged him. What she'd come here tonight to say wasn't going to be easy. The urge to blurt it out nearly overpowered her, but that sort of shock couldn't be good for a man who'd suffered a stroke a little over a week ago.

"I heard the opening of your restaurant was a resounding success," he said as they sat down at the large dining table.

Only two places had been set. To Harper's relief, they weren't at opposite ends of the twenty-foot table. Her mother would be horrified if she discovered that Harper had shouted the tale of her infidelity from one end of the dining room to the other.

"It went very well. The reviews had nothing but wonderful things to say. You were right to suggest I approach Ashton."

"I had a feeling you two would be good for each other."

Unexpectedly, Harper flashed back to their two nights at the tent camp and felt heat rise in her cheeks. "How come?"

"He's a hugely talented chef and the adventurous sort. You've always been an armchair globetrotter too focused on the future to have fun in the present. I thought he might benefit from your knack of focusing on the finish line and you might give him an opportunity to surprise you."

Her grandfather had nailed what had happened between her and Ashton. "How did you know?"

"You don't think I'm this successful in business because I'm a lucky devil, do you?" Her grandfather offered her a crafty smile. "Did you ever wonder why, after you worked so hard to learn the business, I still went ahead and created the contest between you, Violet and Scarlett?"

Since her grandfather was laying his cards on the table, she might as well play hers, as well. "Because you weren't sure I was the best choice?"

"I knew you were the best choice. I just wasn't sure you knew it."

Harper had little trouble following his logic. "I never really believed I was going to be CEO. I wanted it very badly and worked hard to make sure you approved of me."

"I more than approve of you, Harper. I want you to succeed me."

She had to state the obvious even though it exemplified the lack of confidence her grandfather had just criticized about her. "I'm the only one left standing as far as the contest goes. Scarlett has returned to acting part-time. Violet intends to stay in Las Vegas with JT."

"And what do you want?"

His question surprised her. "To be CEO." But she was not as confident as she'd been a month earlier.

"Do you?"

A better lead-in to what she had to confess wasn't going to present itself. "A week ago you asked me what I was doing in Africa." She gathered a steadying breath and tried to calm her agitated pulse. "The truth is, I went looking for my father. My biological father."

Now that she'd made her shocking revelation, she braced herself for her grandfather's outrage. When he continued to eat his steak without reacting, she frowned.

"Why aren't you asking me anything?"

"Did you find him?"

"Yes."

"And?"

"What do you mean, and?"

"I'm assuming you didn't travel that far without some idea of what you expected out of the encounter." He gave her more credit than was due. "Was he pleased to meet you?"

"Not really." She set her fork down and picked up her wine. "He had no idea I existed."

"Your mother never contacted him." A statement. Not a question.

"Why are you so calm about this?" And then it dawned on her. "You knew about my mother's affair and the fact that I wasn't your biological granddaughter."

"Yes."

"You never told me."

"Why should I? You're my granddaughter."

"Not by blood."

"I love you, Harper. You have been my joy for every single one of your twenty-nine years."

"I had no idea you'd feel that way. You went to such lengths to find Violet and Scarlett and make them part of the business. I worried that you didn't have faith in my ability to succeed you."

"Scarlett was unhappy in Los Angeles and her career was sinking fast. What she lacked in business experience she made up for in intelligence and people savvy. Violet deserved better than Tiberius Stone's small-time casino. She knows Las Vegas inside and out and it shows. Her hotel is the most profitable of all three." He grinned. "You're surprised."

She really wasn't. "Would you have picked her if she hadn't taken herself out of the running?"

"No. She might know Vegas, but you understand our entire organization. I need you as CEO." When she didn't immediately speak, he regarded her solemnly. "Unless you decide you no longer want the job."

"In truth, I'm not sure. One of the reasons I went to Africa was because when I learned I wasn't a Fontaine, a part of me was relieved."

"I can understand that. You've put a lot of pressure on yourself."

"Then I met Greg LeDay and I didn't have an aha moment. He wasn't happy to meet me. He had no interest in starting any sort of relationship. There are a whole bunch of people I'm related to that I'll never get to know."

"Give him some time to think about it. He may change his mind."

"I doubt it."

The epiphany she'd expected upon meeting her biological father hadn't happened. She'd been no closer to discovering who she really was. What had changed her was the time she'd spent with Ashton, seeing Africa through his eyes. Those days had given her a deeper understanding of what made her happy.

"All my life I've wanted you to be proud of me," she said. "It's why I worked so hard."

"And I am."

"From things my father said, I knew you wanted a Fontaine to be at the company's helm."

"Now you're thinking that if you take over one won't be?"

"Actually, I'm not sure I'm as ready to be in charge as I thought."

"You want to stay in Las Vegas?"

"No, I think Violet should take over Fontaine Ciel." That would surprise her very capable sister. "I'd like to spend several years consulting in the area of development."

"Let me guess. Traveling the world to determine the best places to expand?"

"Something like that."

"And you think I should stay on in the meantime?"

She smiled. "You and I both know you're not ready to

stop working. Maybe you could try slowing down a bit. Let your staff handle more."

"You're asking a lot of an old man."

"I trust that you have it in you."

At eight in the morning, Batouri's kitchen was a peaceful place. Surrounded by stainless steel, alone with his thoughts, Ashton did the one thing that had saved him for the past twenty years. He cooked.

The five days since Batouri had opened had been hectic ones. He'd been tweaking the menu daily, using the specials to experiment, finding the perfect blend of traditional and unexpected.

He hadn't seen Harper since the night Batouri had opened. She'd gone to New York City and hadn't yet returned. Each day Ashton grew less confident that he'd made the right decision. He'd turned down the Lifestyle Network show, deciding if he wanted to prove how committed he was to her happiness, he'd have to demonstrate it in a big way. Now his hopes that she'd choose traveling with him over living a lie were dwindling.

Despite how things turned out, he was glad he hadn't pressed her to join him. She'd wanted him to. But for him to make such an important decision for her would have brought her back full circle to her current dilemma. What was it Harper wanted for herself?

Almost as if thinking about her had compelled her to find him, Harper stepped into his kitchen.

"I thought I might find you here."

"Where else?"

She looked exactly the same as the first day he'd met her. The unflappable executive with her hair smoothed back into an elegant French roll. Expensive but understated jewelry adorned her slim neck and delicate earlobes. The hem of her designer power suit sliced her kneecaps in half and showed off her toned calves.

Polished. Professional. Perfect.

His heart sank. She'd obviously chosen her future.

"I spoke to my grandfather about taking over as CEO."

"You didn't tell him the truth then."

"No, I told him." She shook her head in bemusement. "Turns out he's known all along."

"Smart man, your grandfather. But I don't know why that surprises me. Look how you turned out."

"I hope you're going to be okay with my decision."

"I will get behind whatever you choose."

"You're going to take the job with the network then?" She looked disappointed.

He decided not to leave her feeling that way for long. "No. I turned them down."

She brightened. "You're going back to *The Culinary Wanderer*. That's wonderful."

"No to that, as well."

"What? I don't understand."

"You were determined to take the CEO job, which meant I couldn't continue traveling with *The Culinary Wanderer* if we were going to be together. But at the same time, you were right about going with the network. They wanted me to become something I'm not."

"What are you planning to do?"

"You suggested that I work on a cookbook. With the success of Batouri, I was considering opening another restaurant in New York, and Vince is exploring opportunities with other networks."

"You've given up your television career to be with me?" She regarded him in confusion. "But why?"

"I realized something these past few days. I no longer feel invincible. Before I met you I had nothing to lose. That's changed."

Harper stood perfectly still while her mind raced. "I don't understand. You had a great deal at stake. *The Culinary Wanderer*. A brand-new cooking show. Batouri."

"Television shows and restaurants will come and go. The only irreplaceable thing in my life is you."

"Me?"

"The woman I love."

"You love me?"

"Hadn't you guessed?"

"When it comes to love, I'm not too well versed on the ins and outs of romance."

"You haven't had much experience." He took her left hand and placed her palm over his heart. "Neither have I, so you'll have to excuse me if I've bungled a few things."

"I suppose it's something we could work on together."

"I'm glad you said that." He reached into his pocket. "Because I want to spend the rest of my life working on it with you. Marry me?"

His eyes were the most brilliant blue she'd ever seen as he gazed down at her. Harper's mouth went dry. Spinning through her head were all the reasons why it would never work between them.

Like her father, he wouldn't be able to stay put for long. He had restaurants in several countries. Traveling for business meant temptation would lurk around every corner. Would they end up like her parents?

Their opposite approaches to decisions—he would be rash and impulsive while she would study and plan—guaranteed they would fight endlessly.

Her tendency to work too much would cause him to get impatient and bored.

"Yes." Not one of her doubts could stand up against the love she felt for this man. "Oh, yes. Scarlett told me make sure you didn't get away and I wholeheartedly agree."

As metal touched her skin, she looked down. Ashton was sliding a large ring onto the third finger of her left hand. Two circles of diamonds, one white, one pale pink, surrounded a pink diamond. It was a unique take on a traditional halo style engagement ring and absolutely…

"Beautiful," she murmured.

"Not nearly as beautiful as the woman who will wear it." He kissed her long and deep. "I love you."

"I hope you still feel that way when I tell you that I'm not taking over as Fontaine's CEO."

"Why not?"

"Because I'm going to travel to cities that don't have a Fontaine hotel to scout locations. Good thing you're going to be free to travel with me because I don't much like the idea of leaving you home alone."

"Interesting that you should bring this up. Remember that idea you had for a travel series on romantic hotel destinations?"

"Did I say romantic?" she teased. "Actually, romantic is probably a great idea."

"Phillips Consolidated Networks agrees with you and they want us to come up with a list of hotels. The more exotic, the better."

"I thought you were done with them."

"Not completely."

"Were you going to run off and do another travel show without me?"

"Of course not. You don't seriously expect that the producers are going to send me to romantic destinations by myself, do you?"

Dismay made her frown. "If you think I'm going to stand by and let you travel to the world's most beautiful places with some gorgeous, charming female version of you…"

His mouth settled over hers, effectively cutting off her tirade. She wasn't quite done fighting and it took several minutes of kissing for her to become sufficiently limp in his arms. When he thought he could get a word in edgewise, he relinquished her lips.

"My darling, I know you perfectly well. There is no gorgeous, charming female version of me as my costar.

There is only the gorgeous, charming female better half of me that is you."

"Me? Starring on television?"

"What do you say?"

"I'm absolutely terrified." She paused, and a broad grin bloomed. "So yes."

"This is going to be a fantastic project." Sweeping her off her feet, he carried her out into the restaurant's dining area. "You. Me. Exotic destinations. Think of all the amazing places we'll make love."

She laughed. "It all sounds very exciting."

And perfect. Because with Ashton's help she'd discovered her passion and the best version of herself. Most days she might still work too hard, but Ashton would be there to remind her to play, as well. Together they would accomplish anything they set their minds to.

When it looked like Ashton intended to carry her out of the restaurant, Harper stopped him. "Wait, I need my *go* bag."

Ashton paused near the door. "You have a *go* bag?"

"Over there by our booth." She pointed over his shoulder.

"Why do you have it with you?"

"So I'll be ready to leave at a moment's notice."

With a disgusted noise, Ashton exited the restaurant, leaving her bag behind.

"Wait, I need that."

"Not right now." With long strides, he carried her past the casino floor and straight to the elevators. "Because the only place you're going is your suite. With me."

And that sounded just right because the biggest adventure of her life was being with the man she loved.

* * * * *

If you loved A TASTE OF TEMPTATION,
pick up the first two stories in the
LAS VEGAS NIGHTS *trilogy from*
Cat Schield

AT ODDS WITH THE HEIRESS
A MERGER BY MARRIAGE

All available now from Harlequin Desire!

SPECIAL EXCERPT FROM

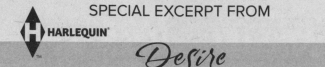

Read on for a sneak peek at **Robyn Grady**'s
TAMING THE TAKEOVER TYCOON,
the fifth novel in Harlequin® Desire's
DYNASTIES: THE LASSITERS series.
The Lassiter legacy is up for grabs, and this means war....

The Robin Hoods of this world were Becca's heroes. As
she watched Jack Reed strike a noble pose, then draw back
and release an arrow that hit his target dead center, the irony
wasn't lost on her.

Jack Reed was no Robin Hood.

Looking *GQ* hot in jeans and a white button-down, Reed
lowered the bow and focused on his guest. The slant of his
mouth was so subtle and self-assured, Becca's palm itched
to slap the smirk off his face.

He freed the arrow from the target, then sauntered over
the manicured lawn to meet her. Although he was expecting
her visit, Becca doubted he would welcome what she had
to say.

She introduced herself. "Becca Stevens, director of the
Lassiter Charitable Foundation." She nodded at the target.
"A perfect bull's-eye. Well done."

"I took up archery in college," he said in a voice so deep
and darkly honeyed the tone was almost hypnotic. "How
may I help you?"

"I'm here to implore you, in J. D. Lassiter's memory, to
show some human decency. Walk away from this."

He laughed, a somehow soothing and yet cynical sound.
"You don't beat around the bush, do you, Becca?"

No time. "You own a stake in Lassiter Media and rumors are rife. People are bracing for a hostile takeover bid. The charity's donations are down. Regular beneficiaries are actually looking at other options. Want to guess why?"

"I'm sure you'll tell me."

Damn right she would. "The name Jack Reed means trouble. Seriously, how much money does one person need? Is this worth betraying your friend's memory? J.D.'s family?"

"This is not about money. And make no mistake." His uncompromising gaze pierced hers. "I intend to win."

Becca's focus shifted from the steely message in his eyes to the arrow he was holding. Then she thought of this man's lack of empathy—his obsession with personal gain. How could this superb body harbor such a depraved soul? How could Jack Reed live with himself?

Becca took the arrow from his hand, broke the shaft over a knee and, shaking inside, strode away.

Don't miss
TAMING THE TAKEOVER TYCOON by Robyn Grady.

Available August 2014
wherever Harlequin® Desire books and ebooks are sold.

Desire

ALWAYS POWERFUL, PASSIONATE AND PROVOCATIVE.

To Catch a Thief, It Will Take a Thief

He comes from a long line of charismatic thieves.
But Gianni Coretti has made a deal to save his
family and now walks the straight and narrow.
When Marie O'Hara, a beautiful security expert,
asks him to steal for her, his interest is definitely
piqued. This is a situation he could make work for
him…in every way.

All he needs is the perfect cover—a gorgeous
fiancée on his arm. Their fierce attraction is only
an added benefit to their ruse. But working so
closely with Marie has Gianni wondering if he'll
ever be worthy. Could a man with such a dubious
past expect to experience a glorious future?

Look for
THE FIANCÉE CAPER
by Maureen Child
next month from Harlequin® Desire.

Available wherever books and ebooks are sold.

HD73330